Wha

"What a delight to read *Reno.* From the first page, I was hooked by Reno's triumphs. As he spends months in his parent's attic recuperating, he is not alone because he has the company of thousands through writing fan letters, listening to sports on the radio, and watching the coming and goings of his neighbours.

Gervais has crafted one of the most vivid and accurate portraits of a twelve-year-old boy that I've ever read. Reno is the boy that I wish I had been at twelve. His lush depiction of 1950s Canada is so detailed in a matter of paragraphs the reader is transported back. The book has a large cast of character, and yet each one, no matter how small a part, is fully realized, which is not easy to do.

Gervais has an impeccable ear for dialogue. And Reno's obsession with Reno Bertoia is completely believable. Read just one page and you too will be touched by Reno."

Robert Hilles, author of *A Gradual Ruin*

"The best of Marty Gervais' work creates an engaging tension between the ordinary surfaces of life and the underlying pathos...."

The Globe and Mail

"Wow! What a wonderful book. So vivid. You really make the characters, the time and place, everything come alive. I too have been working on a polio novel. A little earlier (1953), a very different story (except there was a connection with Huckleberry Finn...I'm amazed that you could write this book in three days. How did you manage that? When did you write it? I think it's one of your best books. Great job."

Robert Hilles, author of *A Gradual Ruin*

"...for him (Gervais), the act of making a poem or telling a story is an act of faith, so that observances of the commonplace become moments of transcendent epiphany and insight, rather than merely journalistic jottings or diaries."

The Oxford Companion to Canadian Literature

"...moving pictures of the past, pictures that resist nostalgia because their themes participate in the present moment. Gervais weaves an anecdotal tapestry whose threads continue to knit through the reader's imagination long after the book has been put away."

Canadian Literature

"...his concerns are with human feeling, laughter, what happens inside the brain when certain lights are turned on."

Al Purdy, Governor General's Award Winner

RENO

Marty Gervais

Library and Archives Canada Cataloguing in Publication

Gervais, C. H. (Charles Henry), 1946-
Reno / Marty Gervais.

ISBN 0-88962-857-2

I. Title.

PS8563.E7R46 2005 C813'.54 C2005-904001-7

Publishing by Mosaic Press, offices and warehouse at 1252 Speers Rd., units 1 & 2, Oakville, On L6L 5N9, Canada and Mosaic Press, PMB 145, 4500 Witmer Industrial Estates, Niagara Falls, NY, 14305-1386, U.S.A.

ISBN 0-88962-857-2

Cover image of Reno Bertoia courtesy of Topps Company Inc, card No. 131, used with their permission.

Mosaic Press in Canada:
1252 Speers Road, Units 1 & 2,
Oakville, Ontario
L6L 5N9
Phone/Fax: 905-825-2130
info@mosaic-press.com

Mosaic Press in U.S.A.:
4500 Witmer Industrial Estates
PMB 145, Niagara Falls, NY
14305-1386
Phone/Fax: 1-800-387-8992
info@mosaic-press.com

www.mosaic-press.com

Courtesy of Topps Company Inc, card No. 131,
used with their permission

Other Books by Marty Gervais

Poems for American Daughter, 1976
Into a Blue Morning, 1982
The Fighting Parson, 1983
Letters from the Equator, 1986
Autobiographies, 1989
Scenes from the Present: New Selected Poems, 1991
People in Struggle: The Life and Art of Bill Stapleton, 1992
The Border Police, 1992
Playing God, 1994
Seeds in the Wilderness: Profile of Religious Leaders, 1994
From America Sent: Letters to Henry Miller, 1995
Tearing into A Summer Day, 1996
The Science of Nothing, 2000
To be Now: New and Selected Poems, 2003
A Show of Hands: Boxing on the Border, 2004

This book is fictional.
Any resemblance to persons living or dead is coincidental. The character of Reno Bertoia, however, is real, but only in name and in those references made to his statistics as a major league baseball player. Anything else related to him is entirely fictional.

Acknowledgements

This book was part of *The 3-Day Novel Writing Contest* and was awarded third prize from Anvil Press in 2002. The book was written at the Windsor Hilton Hotel in an arrangement made with *The Windsor Star* newspaper. Special thanks to Wayne Moriarity, the *Star's* editor at that time, for arranging these accommodations, and taking care of the costs involved and to Judge Saul Nosanchuk who acted as my "referee" during those three days.

I would like to thank John B. Lee, a good friend, poet and writer, who went through this book line by line, and offered advice and guidance.

Marty Gervais,
June 2005

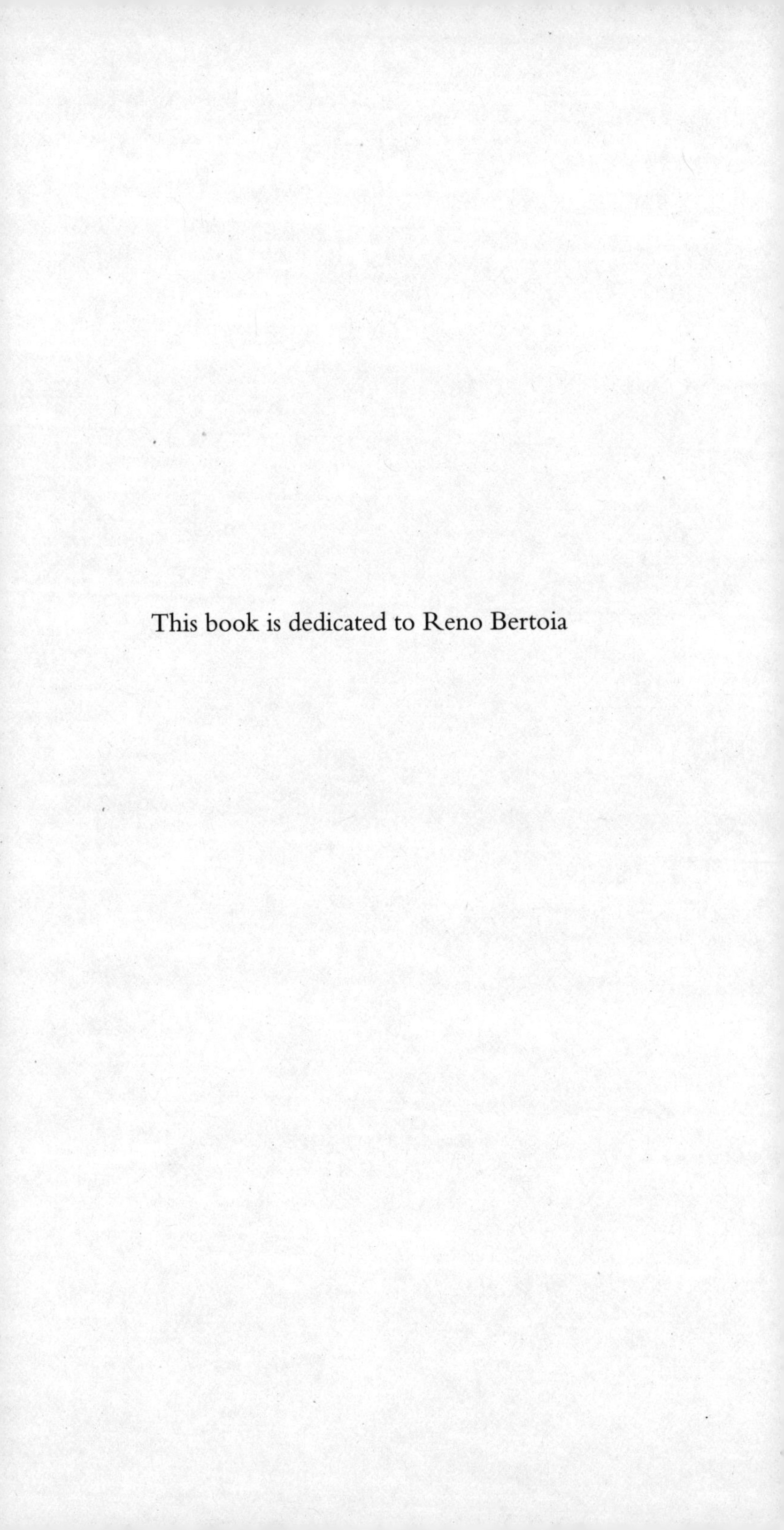

This book is dedicated to Reno Bertoia

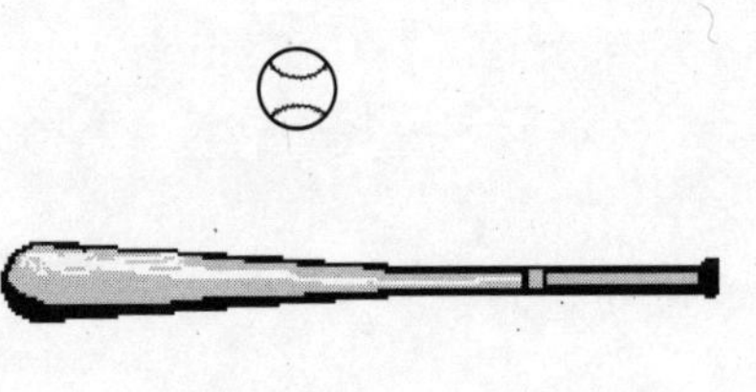

Chapter One

I SAW THE OLD doctor burn down his house that day. He died in the fire. I had seen him that morning conveying a gasoline can from the garage. Moments later his place was ablaze. I don't know why I didn't call the fire department. I just didn't. The smoke billowed and funneled out, like black ghosts from that one-storey bungalow. I thought I might catch sight of the old doctor running out the door. For a time I thought he might've slipped out the back, and I hadn't noticed. As it happened, he never came out at all.

Later when the fire trucks were zigzagged in front of Doc Wellington's house, and neighbours and gawkers filed into the street, I, too, went out. It was early spring, early morning with the milk trucks now chugging back to the dairy after the first runs like defeated linebackers. It was still too cold to venture forth without a jacket. My mother called for me to come back inside. She finally handed me a blanket from the cedar closet. I wrapped myself in it. Inhaling the pungent cedar fumes. Some neighbours were surprised to see me because I had been sick for a long time. I had polio. I was now on the mend. I still had difficulty walking, but I didn't care — I yearned for my freedom. I seized every opportunity to sneak a peak at the outside. And when I did step out, mothers would whisk away their children, fearing their sons or daughters might catch this polio. None did. As it would turn out, I would be the only case in the town.

Most days were spent in the attic, surveying this vacation community of 2,900 people. I knew everyone's name. I made a point of reading about them each week in the *Gazette*. I knew about all the charities, the ladies auxiliaries, the Rotarians, the Jaycees, the Lions club, the card clubs, those at the Curling Rink, the chancel guild at the Anglican Church. I knew the habits of everyone in town. Their obsessions. The kinds of cars they favoured. I could spot the businessmen going to the post office in the morning to pick up parcels. Could see them lolling about to gab in the warm sunshine of a new day. I would imagine their conversations. Imagine their lies. Imagine their dreams. How many children they'd have before they died. At 12, perhaps, I didn't understand any of it. Maybe now as a grown man, I probably have enlarged upon the truth. That's okay. Why not? I spent enough time in that attic room looking out over the town like a sea captain straining his eyes over the frigid steel-gray sea.

Mostly, I think, I fantasized about what it would be like to be normal again.

I knew no one in the town. That is, I had not met any kids my age. We had moved there in late fall after my birthday. I could spy these boys down at the town park, playing touch football in the open field near the band shell. My mom had promised that by next fall, I'd be ready for school, that I'd be able to play down there. I kept my focus fixed on turning 13 next year. Maybe getting a chance to play hockey for the first time in more than a year. Maybe meeting a girl.

We moved to this town because my father was transferred here. In Windsor, I had lived on a street across from a school. My best friend lived right next to the school. Every morning, my routine had been the same. I'd get up, slurp down a bowl of hot oatmeal, head across to my buddy's house where Joanie — his mom — would set out a plate of bacon and eggs. She was a doll. I loved her. As I thought about that in the attic, I wished I had stayed in Windsor. Even when I started getting sick, she'd come across to my house, stop at the back door, and call me through the screen. "Hey, Hank! I've got something for you!"

The aroma of bacon and eggs wafting in the morning air.

Back then I couldn't move from my bed. I was too sick. Yet I still had an appetite. Then I'd hear the screen door slap behind her, as Joanie tiptoed through the kitchen and into the back bedroom where I lay. My mom sitting there beside me. I'd watch her fuss with her hair, curls falling limply across her forehead.

"Oh, Joanie, you shouldn't!"

Always the same words.

"For my Hank — I sure miss him in the morning!" She then would hand me the plate. And tease me: "Hank, how's the arm? You ready to strike out the next batter?"

All these years later, I feel badly thinking of her. For a long time, she sat alone in a Windsor nursing home. Her family — my best buddy from childhood there — rarely bothered to visit. I, myself, only stopped in once. I didn't even recognize her. Gone was that old vibrancy. The eyes were sunken, gloomy, lifeless, lacking in hope. I couldn't believe it was the same woman from my childhood. That vivacious, charming woman, who had been a flapper in the '20s, a woman who made me laugh. The same woman who cared for nothing in the way of protocol when it came to my illness. She was there to give me breakfast each day before we left for this town.

The last time I saw her in the nursing home, she seized my wrist and implored me to return. She trusted me, now that I was a doctor. I promised I would. I never did. I'd drive right past the nursing home. I'd promise myself I would return. I never did. Why? I don't know. I simply never went back. At her funeral a few years ago, I knelt in front of the casket and whispered: "Joanie, I'm sorry — I should've come to see you!"

That's what we do. We make promises. We say things we don't mean. We do things we don't mean. We wind up wishing we could change it all. We never do.

Maybe, that's why I'm writing this now. To make sense of it all. To make sense of those years in the attic when I perched myself on a stool by the window to gaze out over that town. To make sense of those weeks in April, May and June of 1957. Those weeks when I lived on hope. On what came in the mail. On what I heard on the radio.

That time in the attic. The long days. Many of which I cherished. I had the perfect vantage point of the town. I remember years later picking up a postcard from the First World War era. A hand-coloured photograph of this town — the clock tower, post office, the main street with its sloping hill, the dairy with the horse-drawn wagons. Across the top of the card were the words, "A Bird's Eye View …"

That, I thought, is what that view was. That panorama from the attic. A bird's eye view. From there, I could recognize Mrs. Thomas making her way downtown. Two minutes after nine in the morning. She'd nod to Bill

Bradley, the florist who was out sweeping the walk in front of his narrow little shop. He'd straighten up and greet Mrs. Thomas. I imagined she'd say something like, "Good morning, Mr. Bradley! Maybe some rain today?"

"Oh, no! I heard the report. Cloudy this morning. Sunshine this afternoon!"

"Oh, that's good news!"

And she'd go on.

The same conversation without variation, day in, day out.

Then I'd peer down the street from another window. See Russ at the Shell Station, shambling out to pump gas. Or Lum Bailey at the dairy. Catch him sliding heavy wooden crates into the trucks. Sometimes, I'd get up before dawn, and see the drivers loading up. Hear their laughter. Then watch the lumbering trucks — exhaust trailing in the cold, crisp, Muskoka air morning.

Sometimes I'd pretend I was a puppeteer. I held the strings. I controlled the destiny of these people. These were my characters in a play. I offered them life. Governed their movements. Furnished them words. Gave them anger, and joy and laughter and jealousy. Gave them success and failure, love and hate. I made them squabble. I made them swear. I made them run. I made them tell lies. I made them confess. I made them sick. I made them grieve. I made them pay attention to one another. I made them say they were sorry. I made them live in my world, on my terms. I was God.

Then I'd cry. Tears streamed down my cheeks. I'd cry because I knew it was all a lie. I could do nothing here. Except peer into their lives. And dream. Dream that I'd be playing with the boys in the park, running alongside them next to the movie theatre.

I used to see the boys. I knew their names because my father knew their fathers, and because I pestered my Dad for weeks to see if he could find out their names, and determine how old they were. My father returned with it all written out: "I think I have it straight now," he'd say. I pored over those names. Memorized them. The problem was I didn't know who was who. That was okay. I had the names. Then I'd strive to match them up. That has to be Barry. That one, James. Or Bruce. And so on.

A game of names.

That's also about the time I changed my own name. I hated "Henry." Never liked the name. Mostly because of that popular — and very stupid — Paramount television series where Alice would call "Hen—r-y! Hen—r-y! Hen—r-y Aldrich?"

So I changed my name to Reno.

I heard that name on the radio from the summer before we moved here. I had tuned in a ball game and heard the announcer: "Now coming in to play third base is Reno Bertoia … He's from across the river in Windsor."

That's all I needed. He was from Windsor. I was from Windsor.

Then again from the announcer: "This young feller grew up on the sandlots over there … Got his chance with the Tigers — he hasn't played much, but, let me tell ya, he can do some magic with that glove!"

"Reno, it'll be," I thought. Yet I knew nothing about this ballplayer. Nothing at all. I also had no particular interest in the game itself, although I played it at school.

Nothing organized. Just batting around the ball, or hurling an Indian rubber ball against the south wall of the school at dusk.

"R-E-N-O," I sounded out the letters. Liked the timbre. Heavy and rich like the cream on top of milk in bottles on frosty spring mornings.

The name also seemed meaningful and important.

That night, I told my Mom. "For now on, I want to be called 'Reno.'"

"Don't be silly!"

"No, Mom! That's my new name!"

It didn't matter. She still called me Henry. Always would.

Years later after I finished school in that town up north, I switched back to my old name. But in school in this new town, everyone called me "Reno." Indeed, whenever my classmates encountered my family and overheard them refer to me as "Hank," they'd look surprised. They felt that the name "Henry" or "Hank" never suited me. I was a "Reno."

So, for a brief time in my childhood, that's who I became. Reno, it was. Even my tutor called me that. That's probably the only thing I liked about Mrs. Williams. I lamented those fall and winter mornings when she'd come to the house to assist me with my studies. I hated this woman. Hair pulled back tightly and tied. Arms hairy and large like a workman's. She also had a whisp above her top lip. I used to sketch cartoons in the margins of the textbooks of a woman with a Groucho Marx mustache. She never caught on. Or maybe never noticed, or cared. I hated her. Each Tuesday and Thursday. Stopping first thing in the morning. I had warned my mom I wanted Mrs. Williams gone before lunch, before Soupy Sales came on. I looked forward to sitting in front of the television with my soup and sandwich to chuckle at his slapstick antics. Black Tooth and White Fang. I'd attempt the Soupy Shuffle, but could never get it right. My legs buckled. My mother frowned. I could see why — she'd have to put up with the nocturnal stirrings when she'd wake to rub my sore legs. I'd lie there, endeavoring to hold back the pain, all the while her hands massaged my limbs, stiff as boards. Finally, I'd fall back to sleep. At times, my mother, too, would nod off — her head resting by my legs. I know because I'd open my eyes, and find her there. I felt sorry for her.

Often I'd catch her sitting by the kitchen window, alone in the afternoon, with a cup of tea. She had been crying. I'd ask what was bothering her, and she'd wave me away with a piece of dampened tissue. "Nothing, nothing!" She feared the worst with my polio. The doctor told her things were on the mend — I was getting better and I'd be back in school in September. I could now get around. Yet there still was so much fear among the town's people. Maybe that's what bothered my mom. Maybe it was how people avoided us. They didn't want to go near our house. They didn't want their children coming by. Maybe, too, she understood my loneliness — those long mornings and afternoons spent in the attic.

Yet it was my choice to sleep there. To be there. My parents had wanted me to sleep across the hallway from them. I chose the attic instead — the sprawling, low, slanted-ceiling room with the windows facing east and west along the main street. I could see the Norwood Theatre, the marquee advertising Burt Lancaster in *Gunfight at the O.K. Corral*. The ads in the *Gazette* were tantalizing: "Lancaster...famed lawman ... with Kirk Douglas, feared gambler bad guy ...in a strange alliance that reached its climax, that deadly day in Tombstone!"

I could see the clock tower of the old post office. Its big face like the sun or the moon's blissful visage in a children's book. Its benevolent countenance. I'd sit up in my bed and nod to it like the men and women acknowledging a good neighbour on the main street. It was comforting. I also used it to record details. The exact movements of town's people. Simeon the barber. Without fail, ten after nine every morning. Unlocking the shop on the hill. The diminutive white-brick barbershop that clung to the slant of the street. Every Monday, he'd park his car in front of the shop and haul in canvases. My father told me he painted landscapes. The barbershop walls — as I would discover in due course — were crowded with these pictures. Bright beautiful Muskoka landscapes. All seasons. Simeon's tiny shop, I would later learn, reeked of hair tonics and oil paints. A potpourri of odours. The irony was he never once ventured out to the lakes he painted. It was all from memory. The lakes, all illusory. The barns, boathouses, wobbly, cedar docks that angled out into the dark foreboding lakes, all in his mind. Simeon was British. Emigrated here after the First World War. Settled in the town. Started cutting hair. And sold his paintings to customers.

His routine never varied.

The same with everybody else. I'd gaze at the clock. Check the time. There would be Paul, the taxi driver, stopping by the Lakeview Diner, right across from the movie theatre. Strolling back out with a steaming coffee filled to the brim. The big dumb smirk on his face. Everybody believed he was a millionaire. There he was: 9:22 every morning. Same every day. Except Sundays when he'd pull his cab up to St. Thomas's Anglican Church. His children and wife piling out. And Paul, finally stepping out and idling there on the street to straighten his tie, and he'd lean down to check it in the reflection in the taxi's window.

I loved the attic. Though it was difficult getting downstairs. My father installed another handrail after I insisted upon staying up there. It would certainly have been easier to be down one floor. But I had been getting better at this, so they permitted me to move from the second floor to the third. Besides, I had learned an effective way of going down. I'd sit down, and descend the stairs one step at a time on my bum. Later when I had more strength, I'd use the handrails and brace myself, again moving one step at a time, pacing myself. It was difficult, but I was determined to be there. It was the attic that I wanted.

My mom would carry snacks up there. She'd bring milk and toast. And pills. An endless supply of multi-coloured pills. All sizes. I could never pronounce their names. I called them simply, Andrew, Billy Charlie and Frank. A, B, C, and F.

It was there on the third floor of this big house on the main street that I listened to the radio. It opened up a new world for me. In Windsor, I had only watched television. Never paid much attention to the radio, though I recall my mom ironing, and laughing with Art Linkletter in the afternoons.

When I moved north, and finally convinced my parents it would be fine for me in the attic, I discovered an old Zenith radio left behind from previous owners. I plugged it in, and it worked. The first sound from this white plastic box was Jimmie Rodgers singing *Honeycomb*. But music wasn't what interested me. Though I did delight in Elvis and Pat Boone and the Everly Brothers who sang *Wake Up Little Susie*.

It was hockey and baseball that I began to tune in. It's what got me started on the letters.

CHAPTER TWO

I WOULD BE 13 NEXT fall. I'd be going into Grade 8 if I passed. I didn't really have any idea how I was doing. The textbooks I was using were borrowed from the school. The tutor brought them to the house. She said eventually someone from the school would have to test me. She also warned my parents I was really falling behind and I probably wouldn't be going into Grade 8. I despised this witch. She had nothing good to tell me. I'd stay up in the attic, and refuse to come down. Of course, I had an excuse. I was sick.

I dreaded the footsteps of this woman on the creaky wooden staircase to the attic room.

"Hello Reno!" she'd call up.

"HAL-LOW!" I'd call back sarcastically.

She disliked my attitude. And so it would go. This mutual distaste for one another.

I learned nothing. I learned more from gazing outside. I knew things even about her. Or imagined them. I'd follow her from my window. See her wend her way down to Giles Bowman's workshop behind his home. He was a monument carver. And there would be my tutor, strolling into Bowman's workshop. A few minutes later, Bowman would emerge with Mrs. Williams. Arm in arm. To the house. The "closed" sign placed neatly in the shop window. I could never tell how much time they spent in the house because Soupy was on.

Mrs. Williams was married to George, a foreman at the lumber mill at the edge of town. He worked sometimes 15 hours a day. She also did tutoring at night. Bowman was married too. His wife, Julie, worked at the registry office. At night, she was involved with the church choir and on weekends, the chancel guild. At 12, I didn't care what people did. I wasn't even remotely interested in whether it was right or wrong. It was purely something I saw going on. I never judged it. I never cared really. Mostly what mattered to me was the radio. I'd spend hours tuning in baseball and hockey games. Or fights out of Detroit or New York. Like the Jan. 2 fight between Sugar Ray Robinson and Gene Fullmer. I kept twisting the dial till I found it. Fifteen rounds. Fullmer triumphed over the weaving and quick footwork of Robinson. Couldn't get it on television. Only one channel up here. Only the Leafs. Except for the Stanley Cup finals. Then it was always the Canadiens. I loved Montreal. Loved the Rocket. My body would tense up as I listened to the raspy radio voice of Danny Gallivan. His emotions rising every time the Rocket rushed to the net … I loved hockey. But only ever got to play road hockey. Now I couldn't even do that. I cursed my legs some nights. I dreamed of being a hockey player. Dreamed of skating in the Forum, yearned for the thundering applause. Dreamed of rushing down the right wing with the Rocket, but knew he had to be an old man now … It was 1957. I'd lie in my bed in the darkness of the attic, tune in the radio, the Cup finals fading in and out with Gallivan's voice … I cursed my radio for failing me.

That night in January, Robinson was defeated. I nearly missed two rounds, as the radio dipped in and out. What mattered to me the most was this radio. Nothing else in town. With it, my mind soared beyond smoke stacks and rooftops. I could touch down in the Boston Gardens where the Rocket terrorized the goalies, and where the Habs rolled in like thunder to wreak havoc on the Bruins. And they did. Four out of five games, thrashing them like there was no tomorrow … I cheered from my bed. And the night they won the Cup, my mother rested beside me on the edge of the bed, massaging my sore legs— they had ached all day long …It was Dickie Moore who scored the winner in that fifth game. Fourteen seconds into the second period. Rocket had done it the year before.

The radio had taken me there. To that moment. Years later when I went to the Forum with my son, it was as if I had been there, had stood there among the crowd. It was so familiar. I stood along the rail, and watched the great Lafleur fly over the blue line and plant the puck in the top right hand corner of the net. The old building thundering under the feet pounding of fans and the infectious chanting of "Guy! Guy! Guy! Guy!" Almost scary.

The radio was what lifted me from this room. Transplanted me. Lowered me down in the smoky arenas of Madison Square Gardens where Robinson battled for the middleweight title, or in the cold red wooden seats of the Forum where all the men wore shirts and ties to the games … I loved turning off the light in my room. Luxuriating in the isolation of it. The radio. Companion. Friend.

That's what led me to the letters.

I first wrote to the Rocket. Addressed it to the Montreal Forum. Got back a black and white picture of him in return. Autographed simply, *Maurice Richard #9*.

That's not what I had expected. I had written him a letter. I had things to say.

Dear Mr. Richard:

I listen to you on the radio. I knew your Canadiens would win the Stanley Cup this year. You are the greatest hockey player of all time, even though some say Gordie Howe is better. Not in my books!

I have a question: What is your secret when you are coming in on the net on a breakaway, when it's just you and the goalie? How do you know what to do?

Reno

The Rocket never wrote back. I pinned the autographed picture above the small wooden desk my father built for me.

Then I wrote to Gordie Howe.

Dear Mr. Howe

I watched you on television one night when you were playing the Leafs. You picked up the puck just over the red line. No one could catch you. But everyone was right there! They could've caught you. You didn't outskate them. You just held on to the puck in a mysterious way. I asked the priest about that. I told him that you probably sold your soul to the devil! I looked at your records, and you weren't any good in that first year. You did nothing to impress anyone. Suddenly you're a great hockey player, though I don't think you are as great as the Rocket! What happened? Did you make a pact with the Devil?

Reno

Two weeks went by. I received an envelope from Detroit. I let it sit in the foyer near the front door downstairs for a day before I dared opening it. When I finally got up the nerve – you see, I was embarrassed by what I had written — I used a butter knife to slice open the end of the envelope. There inside was a black and white photograph of Howe on the ice at Detroit's Olympia. Across his legs in ink were these words: *To my friend, Reno, all the best! Gordie Howe.*

Nothing about the devil!

I was relieved. I pinned his picture above my desk in the attic, alongside the Rocket. Two colossal figures in the NHL. The vanquishers of reputations.

Some afternoons, I'd stare at these two giants. Study their eyes. Sometimes I'd unfix them from their place above my desk, and hold them apart and pretend they were alive in my hands, imagining them on the ice, as I skated them on the broad surface of my desk, this surface now being the Forum. I'd become Danny Gallivan, doing the play-by-play. The swift Rocket would always win, always get past the elbows of the expeditious Mr. Howe.

I'd play like that for a long time, and often fall asleep, the pictures limp in my hands, my face flat on the hard desk. My mother would rouse me, pin the pictures back, and help me to the bed. Again, rubbing my legs. Straightening them. The stiff hurt legs of my childhood. The legs I dreamed would outskate everyone in the NHL, except maybe the Rocket. I had so much affection for him. And hated Geoffrion for taking away his scoring title! I dreamed of that wide sweep the Rocket would make around the defense, how he would hurtle toward the net, his face ablaze. I'd tell my mom, "Some day I'll be there, mom! With him!"

I wrote to Richard again.

Dear Monsieur Richard

You are the greatest! Do you think if you and Gordie Howe each took a puck at the same time from centre ice and skated in opposite directions on two different goalie (both of equal talent), that you'd make to the other end first and score? I think you would!

Reno

At the end of April I got a package in the mail. The return address was the Montreal Forum. Again, I meticulously sliced open the flap of the envelope with the butter knife taken from the kitchen drawer.

Another picture. The same picture of Richard. Blazing eyes, the puck on his stick.

His autograph. This time: "A mon ami, Reno — Maurice Richard."

I pinned it above my desk. Alongside the other picture of the Rocket. Two Rockets. One Gordie Howe. "Two to one," I giggled. "You win, Rocket!"

That winter I also wrote a letter to Sugar Ray Robinson. I never got anything in return. I had told him in the letter that he'd win the next fight. He was 36 years old. That seemed so old. I told him he still had that unmistakable quickness.

Sugar Ray never wrote back. I kept looking for a letter to arrive, especially because I had received three from the Rocket and Howe.

But nothing came.

I wrote to Rocky Marciano too. But nothing. I had seen him on the Ed Sullivan Show. But again, nothing came back. No answer.

That winter, I dashed off other letters to athletes. But I was striking out. Meanwhile, the pictures of the Rocket and Howe remained above my desk.

Mrs. Williams told me one day that maybe it's because I had nothing to say in these letters, and that's why I wasn't getting anything back. I didn't believe that. And I continued to write. Wrote to David Jenkins, the men's world champion figure skater. Another to Ted Williams. Another to Andy Williams, and Frankie Avalon. Nothing. Nothing.

I was hurt. I thought maybe Mrs. Williams was right after all. I decided I'd tell these stars that I was 12. Maybe then they'd be kinder, and write back. I also thought I might mention I had polio. Then dismissed that notion. They'd start feeling sorry for me — I didn't want that!

For weeks, I wrote nothing at all. I had just about given up until I tuned into a game from Detroit. I heard the name Reno Bertoia. My luck would change.

CHAPTER THREE

ERNIE HARWELL'S VOICE crackled over the airwaves. That familiar deep voice. Reno was in the lineup. I had almost forgotten about him, having been so caught up in hockey, and the Stanley Cup. The radio hummed with the sounds of baseball. But from Florida. The Tigers in spring training. I had always wanted to see a real game. My cousin in Windsor had told me all about Briggs' Stadium at Michigan and Trumbull in Detroit. "You won't believe the *green*," he said. "You won't believe it when you see it — you'll walk along these old corridors, almost as if you're underground, then you'll turn up a ramp, and it's there. *Green! Green!*"

I tried to imagine that, as I listened to the game. One late afternoon in April. A Saturday. Suddenly I heard the bells from the church. I peered down to see St. Joseph's Church, the cars, gleaming that afternoon, the men in tuxes, and a radiant bride standing on the fresh new grass of spring. The *green* of it! So lush. I imagined Briggs Stadium. Like that. I forgot about the game as I watched the newly weds cavorting on the grass. The brownie camera of a parent capturing this moment. A father, or uncle moving back, his arms waving others out of the picture. He peered down to the viewfinder of the camera, shifting the black box cupped in his hands till he got the two of them in the picture. Snap. Crank the winder. Snap. Crank. Snap.

A day in the spring. I imagined myself at Briggs. Imagined digging in at home plate, at driving one down third, and reaching first and moving the runner to second.

Nothing heroic. Just the feeling of a base hit. Something to show. Then standing there at first looking up at the crowd, the score board. Trying to get the edge. To get some momentum. To make something happen on this day in the spring when a win is a win and nothing else matters.

Then Ernie's voice: "That one is L-O-N-G G-O-N-E!"

It was Reno. A blast over the right field fence. The short side. I can see Reno rounding the bases. And Harwell's voice: "That boy's from Windsor, right across the river from Detroit! First homer of the spring season. This is someone you can't underestimate. He's got hitting power. He's got magic in that glove of his!"

Suddenly the car horns started … The wedding. I saw a big lustrous Dodge. Remembered the ads: *Slip into the driver's seat, feel that travelling urge … Then, take off! You'll soon know Dodge is the nimblest number that ever swept over the land, the quickest scataway, the smoothest ride …*

A brand new 1957 Dodge. The one with the "D" button to start.

I was fascinated by advertisements. Recited all the television jingles. Set to memory the ads in the paper. Drove my parents crazy with this stuff. My father complaining, "You waste your time away remembering such useless information!"

Yet I couldn't memorize a line of poetry to save my soul.

I hated my studies. Mostly, I hated Mrs. Williams. I had hoped she wouldn't come anymore. I made life miserable for her. One morning, I deliberately knocked her coffee mug over, spilled the contents onto her dress. She rushed to the bathroom, then came back and made me mop up everything from the floor. I chortled to myself. I had no use for her. I begged my mom to find someone else.

That afternoon of the wedding, I decided I might write another letter. This time to Reno. The next day, however, my mom had other plans. After mass that Sunday — I couldn't attend church — we drove to Midland. It took about an hour and a half in my father's two-toned Plymouth Stratochief with the big fins. My mother told me they were looking for a cure.

Chapter Four

I was improving. So, why did I have to go to Midland? Why there? To the Martyr's Shrine. The relic of Jean de Brebeuf. I saw the crutches, the leg braces. It was spooky. My mom told me to pray. We sat in the front pew. A priest met us there. We sat together. He blessed me. Told me miracles were possible.

"Will I be able to play hockey?"

"Anything is possible my son, if you believe!"

"Believe in what?" I asked. "God?"

"Yes, of course, but also the power of God. In a miracle."

"I'll be healed. I'll be able to play hockey? To skate?"

I wanted to believe him. But in the back of my mind,

I wondered why God would bother with me. Why did I have polio? What was the point of giving me polio?

Still, I said all the *Our Fathers* and a half a dozen *Hail Marys.*

We drove back. My legs ached. I lay on the back seat. The sun over the trees along the highway. I fell asleep. I dreamed of Briggs Stadium. My perfect legs rounding the bases on a summer day. The crowds leaping to their feet. I could run! Lightning fast.

I woke with my father opening the door and reaching in to help me. His glasses reflecting the main street. A car passing by. A boy standing in front of the real estate agent's office. A boy about my age.

"Dad, just a minute!"

He stood up.

"What's wrong?" my Dad asked.

"Oh, nothing … Is there a boy across the street?"

I could see my father straightening up and looking over the top of his Plymouth.

"Uhah!"

"Is he my age?"

"Could be. He's about your size."

"Could you wait till he goes away."

My father hesitated, then agreed. "Sure." He then reached into his shirt pocket under his jacket, pulled out a pack of Player's. Slid one out, and lit it. Dragged deeply on the cigarette, turned slightly to look down the street, as if he hadn't noticed the boy who just kept standing there. Then turned to my mother who had joined him at his side. He told her to go to the house — he'd be there in a minute.

"Is he gone?"

"Nope."

After a moment or two, the boy started down the street toward the A & P. And my father reached down. Smiled. Assured me everything was fine now.

"You shouldn't be embarrassed. You're just not well. But you will be!"

"Will I be cured, Dad?"

"I don't know."

His cigarette bobbed in his mouth as he spoke. He helped me from the car. Told me again, as he did every day. "The leg braces will help, you know. You should wear them when we go out!"

"I don't need them." I said emphatically.

It was good to be back in the attic. My mother had given me a rosary. The priest blessed it, and exhorted me to pray the rosary each night before going to bed. I was unhappy after that visit. Up till then, my focus had been on the radio and the letters and Reno Bertoia.

I asked my father that night before sleep if he had ever heard of Reno Bertoia.

"Yeah, sure. He lived in our neighbourhood. On Hickory Road."

"Really?"

"Yeah, I used to see him all the time. A big lanky kid. Big hands. He used to be an altar boy at St. Angela's Church. That's where we used to go before we moved to Riverside. You wouldn't remember that — you were a baby.

"Yeah, I remember him. I never knew anything about the baseball thing … But he was good. At least that's what everybody told me … I think he was born in Italy. Reno's father, as I recall, worked for Ford's."

"I can't believe that!" I said. "You *knew* Reno Bertoia!"

"Well," my father stammered, "I didn't actually *know* him. I mean, I saw him. He was at church, and he played in the vacant lots … I'd see him out there. You know, he used to live next door to Hank Biasatti …So, you know…"

"Who's that?"

"You mean Hank Biasatti?"

"Yeah."

"Oh well, he was a big number, Played ball for the Philadelphia Athletics."

"Was he good?"

"I guess … Anyway, Reno apparently learned from him. He was called 'A bonus baby!'"

"What's that?"

"He was signed with the Tigers a few years ago when he was 18. Had a big bonus. Even got the Tigers to send his mom to Italy."

"You knew him?"

"Well, as I say he used to play at Stodgell Park on the diamonds there. People didn't pay much attention to him, but the scouts did…"

That night I fiddled with the radio in my room. A stupid song by Perry Como. *Round and Round.* Catchy but stupid, I thought. I hated that song. I twirled the dial. Another song. *That'll be the day* with the Crickets. I fell asleep with that. I had promised I'd write Reno a letter. Tell him what my dad said.

CHAPTER FIVE

THE MONSIGNOR WAS AT my house the next morning. Heard him ascending the stairs to the attic. His big hulking frame. A fat old priest. Wearing a cassock. Hiking it up like a dress. Puffing and puffing up the steps.

"Reno!" he bellowed.

Then emerging from the staircase. His large frame. Silhouetted against the windows. The shock of white hair. "How are you doing son?"

"Good, I guess. Good."

"Feeling better?"

"Well, I don't know — about the same."

He came over to my bed. Sat at the edge of it, the mattress sagging dramatically under his weight.

"I heard you went to the Martyr's Shrine. Your father asked me to have a talk with you."

"You mean, about the cure!"

With that, the monsignor laughed. "Yes, yes … the cure! That will come in time, I'm sure! But no, I'm here to talk to you about Reno."

"You mean, me?"

"Well, yes and no … I want to talk to you about Reno Bertoia."

"You know him?"

"Yes, of course … You see, I used to be a Basilian priest and lived in Michigan when Reno went to Northwestern. My best buddy was Father Ron Cullen, and that was Reno's coach, his mentor really. Anyway, Father Cullen and I had been to the seminary together. At St. Mike's in Toronto.

"Anyway, I knew Reno. Used to watch him play ball. Class D in those days.

"I miss baseball … I don't even listen to the games anymore, but at one time, that's all I wanted to do … I was at Briggs Stadium in Detroit to watch the Tigers go after the series! I was a young seminarian, and I used to wear a cassock, much like this, and they'd let us in."

"But what about Reno?" I persisted. "Did you see him play?"

"Oh yeah, but never in the majors. He played in the sandlots and at school. He played second base, and I was always amazed at how quick he was, moving that ball over to first, doing the double play … And he could hit. Not a slugger, but a down the line hitter, looping Texas Leaguers …He was good!"

I listened to the old priest tell me about Reno. He sat there for a long time. We also talked about my legs. And the cure. The priest told me not to think about that. Told me if God wanted to cure the polio, that would happen. I asked him why God wouldn't want that for me.

"The cure might not be in God's plan," he said.

"But why not?"

He didn't know.

"Don't worry. God will take care of you. Things will work out," he said sadly.

"Will I get to play hockey?"

"I'm sure you will!"

That morning, Mrs. Williams didn't come. She had the flu. I sat in the window surveying the town. I was going to write that letter to Reno.

Reno to Reno.

Cute.

He might think that was neat. He might write back. I might get more than a photograph. I thought I might tell him about the monsignor, my dad, the neighbourhood and Stodgell Park, even though I knew nothing about it. Except what my dad told me.

That morning, I noticed Lillian Lee. A warm day that spring. She wore a pencil-slim skirt, a cardigan buttoned up the back. Loose wavy hair brushed at the sides. My mom always said she acted more like a teenager. Less like the young wife she was. Married to a real estate agent. An alcoholic.

She was pretty, this Lillian. A lot younger than my mom. "A looker," my dad said. That always made my mom scowl.

There Lillian was that morning, strolling along Manitoba Street, the main drag, down to the Parkview. Paul, the taxi driver, was there. He noticed her coming, and waited with his coffee while she approached. One hand on the door handle of his cab. Saying something to her. She was laughing. I saw him touch her shoulder, then saw him bow like a chivalrous knight. Why did he do that? She began slapping a hand on her knee as she bent over, and laughing heartily. He stood there laughing too. There they were, standing beside his taxi in the cool sunlit day. Off schedule.

That was always the way with Lillian. Fellows my cousin's age used to stand around leaning on the parking meters. Sick over Lillian. She flirted with everyone. She'd pause and chat with all the young men. What was the big deal? She was pretty, I guess. But so what?

Yet, there was something about her. A looker. Yeah, maybe. At 12, I didn't understand the interest. At 12, I liked Patricia Van de Veer. She had come from Holland. Blonde hair, ponytail, full skirts. I'd see her on the way to school. She knew nothing about me. I got her name from my father who knew her father. He trucked the headlights my father's company made for Ford's in Oakville. I pestered my dad to get her name.

"You little devil!" he teased.

"Dad! What's her name?"

"All right, I'll ask!"

"Don't say it's me that wants to know!"

"Don't worry, I won't … But you like her, eh?"

"Dad!" I said exasperated.

That morning after Lillian made her way downtown, I thought about Patricia.

Maybe I could write her a letter.

CHAPTER SIX

MY MOTHER BROUGHT ME Ovaltine that night. I hated the taste. She claimed it would help me sleep. I didn't want to sleep. I wanted to write more letters. I still hadn't written to Reno Bertoia. I didn't know what to say. I hadn't seen a picture of him. I had no idea of what he looked like. Tall and lanky is all I knew. There was nothing about him in the papers. He was no Mickey Mantle. No Hank Aaron.

Still I wanted to write. That night, I dumped the Ovaltine out the window. That night when everyone was asleep, I stayed up. I wrote to Reno:

Dear Reno

You will notice I have the same name. My real name is Henry. I hate that name. My mom likes it, but I hate it! When I heard your name on the radio, I decided to change it. You got a base hit that day. It's the first time I knew about you.

I spoke to an old priest who knows you, or at least knows Father Cullen, and I guess he helped you quite a bit when you were starting out.

I listen to you when I can get the games in Detroit. You're my favourite!

Reno

That was the last day in April. The Tigers had made their way north to Detroit, out of the Grapefruit League. Again, I checked the mail daily. I pestered my father, "Are you sure you posted my letter?"

"Yes, I'm sure! I'm sure!"

A week went by. I had given up on Reno. I had also written to Louis Armstrong. He had been on the Ed Sullivan Show. I overheard my father saying he was appearing at Dunn's Pavilion in nearby Bala. I liked him, liked the sound, the crazy, deep, raspy voice, the way he held the trumpet.

Dear Mr. Armstrong

I hear that you are coming to Muskoka. That's where I live. I hope by summer I can get out to hear you play. I saw you on the Ed Sullivan Show last week. You are fantastic.

Reno

Then one morning, Mrs. Williams was on the stairs. "Times tables!" she chirped as she emerged in the attic. I hated her. Detested that high-pitched nervous voice.

That morning, however, she came up the stairs with a letter. A large envelope in her hand. Waving it. But pulled it away when I reached out and demanded that she give it to me.

"Not until you can solve these little problems."

With that, Mrs. Williams handed me a sheet of 25 equations. My heart sank. "C'mon, just let me see what I have in the mail!" My tutor held firm. "Not till you do the work!"

So, I sat there beside her, toiling over these equations. One by one. Meticulously penciling in the answers. She finally handed me the envelope. Return address: New York, from Louis Armstrong's agent. I opened it carefully. An autographed photograph. It was only a week. And Armstrong had signed it: "*Satchmo Armstrong*."

I pinned it beside the Rocket and Gordie Howe.

Again no letter.

I wrote more letters. I was branching out. I wrote Yul Brynner. He had just been in *The King and I*. I figured I'd never see the movie the way my illness was going. Besides, we weren't likely to get it at the Norwood. Playing there now was *The Ten Commandments*, and he was in that. Again, I wasn't allowed out. I had to content myself with his photographs in the papers. My father subscribed to both the *Telegram* and the *Toronto Star*. He did it to confuse anyone over his politics. I didn't care — I devoured the papers. Not only the sports sections, but everything. I savoured every word.

That same day I tuned into a game in Detroit.

The Tigers had just started the regular season.

The first of May. Tigers in Detroit. Reno back in the lineup. Twenty-two year old now playing third. Finally getting a chance, after bouncing about between the minors and the majors. Three days into the regular season. And batting .383. I read in the paper what Dick Tighe, the manager said: "He goes up here now with the feeling he can hit anyone in the league — and that's just what he's doing."

Already third in the league in hitting.

"I know. I know," I reasoned. "It's early. It's no big deal."

I cheered from my bed listening to the game. Reno had gone three for four in the game against Baltimore. Williams, the master, going zero for four against the Yankees.

I wrote to Reno again.

Dear Reno

I know you're busy. I wrote you a few weeks ago when you were in Lakeland playing the exhibition games. I have the same name as you, you see. I would love to see you play some day, and when I am better I will make a point of going to Detroit. Maybe with my dad. I am 12 years old. I love your name!

Reno

That same night Sugar Ray kayoed Gene Fullmer to win his fourth title. Fullmer had abandoned the rushing brawling tactics, and the "sweet as sugar" fighter finished him in the fifth round. The papers said Fullmer's approach was like a bull trying to second-guess a toreador.

I wrote to Sugar Ray.

Dear Mr. Ray

I knew you'd win. I told you that you had deadly quickness. Fullmer is all fists but no brains, my dad says! He can't take your speed. Way to go!

Reno

CHAPTER SEVEN

THE FIRST WEEK OF May that year I woke up to the sounds of bulldozers. I struggled from my bed to the window. The doctor's house was being taken down. The garage was already leveled. I wondered what had become of the big yellow De Soto the doctor owned. I didn't remember it being taken away. It had been partly burned in the fire. I was sad to see the bungalow go. I wondered what would be there in its place. The doctor had committed suicide. That wasn't uncommon in this town. Or so it seemed. A man two blocks away who worked at the pool hall was found hanging in the closet of an upstairs bedroom. Someone said he was upset over his wife having had an affair with his business partner.

Another man shot himself. Put a pistol into his mouth and blew his brains out. Upset over losses at Woodbine in Toronto. Had gambled away his life's savings.

A high school student last fall killed herself over a boyfriend.

I sat on my stool near the window, thinking about all this. Sitting there in my pajamas watching the doctor's house bulldozed. What had gone wrong? His wife had died earlier in the year. Everyone said it had been a "loveless marriage." Whatever that means. I didn't know. I guess he didn't care for her. But why kill himself? Was it over her? Some say it was over Suzie, the librarian's daughter, and that he got her pregnant. The old doctor was nearly 65, Suzie, 17. She used to come to the doctor's house on Friday afternoons. She'd stop by to clean, or so it was said. Vacuum, dust, and wash up the dishes. Others claimed the old doctor was having his way with her.

Now, there they were, taking down his house. I wondered about Suzie. I hadn't seen her in a month. Some believed she had gone to Toronto to have the baby.

The old doctor — a laconic and self-absorbed man with white hair — once stopped in to see me about my polio. Curious about it, since no one in the town had contacted it. He took my temperature, listened to my heart, peppered me with questions, then patted me on the head, and mumbled, "You're a good boy!"

That was it.

We had Dr. Ian Black as our family physician. He was familiar with the disease, having treated it in Toronto. He seemed unusually joyous when my mother made an appointment with him. He came to the house. I hated his visits because of his beer breath and sweat. He'd take off his suit jacket, and there would be those ugly, deep, wet armpit stains. I wanted to flee.

Always the same prognosis: *He's getting better. He'll be back to school soon. Don't worry.* After a while I didn't believe him. I hadn't been out of the house, except for a trip to the Martyr's Shrine and a picnic to Algonquin Park and some afternoons of sitting on the shaded back verandah. I hated the garden. I yearned to be free. To make my way down the hill on the main street, past Simeon's barber shop. I had yet to see the interior of it. I had yet to see what the Parkview looked like, though my Dad told me it wasn't much. Some leather booths, gumball machines, great milkshakes. He brought me a chocolate shake almost every Friday.

I yearned to make my way downtown. Down to the wharf where the boys dove into the water. At the foot of the falls. I drove over that bridge a few times with my dad. Spotted the kids tumbling into the water like acrobats off the shoulders of this giant wharf. I wanted to dip my arms and legs and face into the cold Muskoka River. My Dad told me stories of the river. His plant was on property a few miles away. It backed on to the South Branch of the river. Said it ran quicker there, and how a hermit had built himself a shack in the woods. My father could evict him, but he wouldn't. He left the old man alone — he wasn't hurting anybody. So why bother?

I wanted things to change.

My luck would change with Reno. I sensed that. I wrote him again. Now the second week of May. I still hadn't heard anything from him, even though it had not been long.

Dear Reno

Keep up the good hitting! You're going to beat Williams this year!

Reno

I also wrote to Willie Shoemaker. Sent it to Churchill Downs. I felt sorry for the jockey. I saw a photograph in the *Toronto Star* of him riding Nerud. He was standing in the stirrups at the 16th pole. He hadn't realized he hadn't finished the face. He hadn't realized Iron Liege, ridden by Bill Hartack, would regain the lead and steal the Kentucky Derby.

Dear Mr. Shoemaker:

Cheer up!. You did everything right, and you thought you had won, and you would have. Oh, gosh, it must make you feel badly. My mom always says sometimes we do things and we don't know why, then we make mistakes, but it's okay — we're human. It happens. I'm sorry for you, but you know you're good. You know you should have won! In my books, you did win!

Reno

It didn't take the bulldozers long. By late afternoon that day in May the house was rubble. The trucks started hauling away the bricks and charred remains. They say after the fire the firemen found the old doctor leaning up against a kitchen wall, propped up against the charred two-by-fours. He's now buried next to his wife in the cemetery down by the river. Willy's Park they call it.

Chapter Eight

A night game in Detroit. Tuned it in. Reno still battling for first place in hitting. One step behind the faltering Williams.

I still had no word from Reno. Nothing at all.

The other day Williams, riled up over a bad pitch, hurled his bat at the dugout, scattering his own teammates. The bat-flinging incident caught the attention of the umpire, and he reported it to the league. Mickey Mantle did the same earlier in the week.

Meanwhile, Reno kept plugging along.

Joanie in Windsor sent me a letter with a picture of Reno. Fresh face with a big grin. I pinned the newspaper with his head and shoulders picture up beside Louis Armstrong and the Rocket and Gordie Howe. I couldn't believe I had this picture. I finally had something to look at it. It helped me imagine him at Briggs Stadium. I put a face with that imaginary body that I saw racing around the bases when I heard Harwell on the radio. I'd shut my eyes and picture this lanky ballplayer smashing a double to centre field, and how he might round second just a few feet, to get the edge, maybe force the outfielder to make a wild throw into the infield. Then Reno would retreat, content to be at second, content to be playing. I knew he'd do well. I knew he'd show them. I thought I'd like to keep a scrapbook, but the Toronto papers didn't bother to mention him. It was always about Williams, who was still on top, though he was struggling at the plate.

There was an article in the *Windsor Star* that Joanie sent about the meeting of these two. In a game between the Tigers and Boston, Williams had landed on third base with a triple, a sharp hit into the corner that fooled the right fielder. He stood at third, a little out of breath.

"How're you doing, Mr. Williams," asked Reno.

"Not bad, Bush!" Williams apparently said without even looking at Reno.

Apparently the great Williams called everyone Bush.

Again I wrote to Reno.

Dear Reno

You're chasing the old man! You're about to get him! Don't let up.

Your greatest fan, Reno

Still no response. But one day during that week in May there came a letter from the Chuck Berry fan club. I had sent in $2 to join. There arrived a membership card, a newsletter and a photograph of the great performer. I pinned this picture to the growing gallery above my desk. Richard, Howe, Louis Armstrong, Reno, now Chuck Berry.

I spent an afternoon re-arranging their pictures in importance. Rocket on the top alongside Satchmo. Reno and Chuck Berry side by side, Howe at the bottom. I still didn't like him. Still, he called me his friend.

I fell asleep during the game on the radio.

Reno was in Baltimore. Came into the game as a pinch hitter for Jim Bunning, the pitcher. The game had gone into extra innings. Reno struck out the first time up in the 14th, but was back two innings later to smash one into left field and drive in the winner.

I had fallen asleep. But heard about it the next day.

"He's getting close," I thought.

That next day, my dad bought a brand new Studebaker, a long sprawling car with a sweeping back. My mother helped me down the back steps to see it. My dad was leaning back in the upholstered seats. A Player's smoking in one hand, a forearm resting on door with the window down.

"Dad, did you see Reno? He's going to be first in the American League!"

"Really? I didn't know that. If he does make it, it probably won't last long!"

"Oh, c'mon, Ted Williams is an old man!"

"Not as old as I am!" my dad countered.

"No, you know what I mean, Dad — he's played forever, and doesn't have it anymore! He's so mad at Reno — he's tossing bats all over the place. Reno's taking over!"

My father helped me into the car. My mother sat in the back. I sat in the front. I ran my hands over the smooth dashboard, reveling in all the buttons of this two-tone woodsmoke gray and arctic white new car. A V-8 engine. My father at the wheel, still sporting the spotted bowtie, and proudly turning into the near-empty back streets of the town, taking a short cut down to the river road. The car like a dreamboat. The engine humming under the hood. The radio on. Perry Como crooning…

That night I wrote a letter to Perry Como. I didn't like him, but I thought my father did.

Dear Mr. Como

My father loves your voice. I love your cardigans, and I've tried to get my dad to wear one. But he only wears white shirts and bow ties, and on weekends, a sleeveless undershirt. But he loves your songs. So does my mother. I wish you the best of luck with your new song Round and Round ...

Reno

It wasn't long in coming. A letter from RCA in New York. A photograph of Perry Como. Signed: *To Reno, a great young fan! Perry Como.*

I had wanted him to autograph it for my father. And told my dad this after it had arrived in the mail.

"Hey, that's great! You can put that with the others!"

"Dad, I thought you could take it to work with you! You like him so much."

"But Hank, it's autographed to you!"

"Yeah, I know, but —"

"No, you keep it, and whenever I want to see it, I'll know where to find it."

I hated that song of Perry Como's. I didn't even like him. I did this for my dad. Nevertheless, I pinned his picture next to Gordie Howe's. The hockey player who sold his soul to the devil, and the one whose voice I couldn't stand. I had lied — I absolutely couldn't stand those cardigans Como wore!

But up he went. Perry Como. Gordie Howe. The Rocket. Chuck Berry. Louis Armstrong and a faded newspaper clipping of Reno Bertoia.

That night I prayed that Reno would make it to the top. That he'd go right to the end of the season, snagging the wide balls at the hot corner, and knocking in teammates...

CHAPTER NINE

I AM NOT SURE HOW long I had been there in the window, when I spotted the boy I had seen the other day when I was getting out of my dad's old car. He was standing across the street, and looking up at me. When he knew I had spotted him, he waved. I was so shocked, I immediately edged away from the window. I was startled by his candidness. What did he want? Why was he standing there? For how long? How long had it been that I never noticed?

I leaned against the wall, and surveyed my attic hideaway. The unmade bed. The dresser, my clothes hanging in the closet, the leather and steel leg braces propped up in the corner — I didn't wear them much — and the pictures above my desk.

What did he want? Was he still out there?

I moved back toward the window to take a peek. He was still there. Again, I leaned against the wall. My legs bothered me that morning. My mom was at the bank. She had asked if I would be all right. I told her not to worry. I didn't need anything. My dad was at the plant, trying to avert a strike.

Was that boy still there? I didn't know his name. He wasn't one of the boys at the park. He wasn't on the list my dad prepared. Who was he? What was he doing there? I peeked again. He was now leaning up against a tree, still staring up at the attic window. *Who was he?*

That was it — I wasn't going to look anymore. I needed to write a letter. I needed to get up my nerve to write a letter to Patricia. Then I muttered to myself, "What would she think if she got a letter from me? She doesn't even know me."

Patricia had no idea I watched her walking to school. She might think I was weird. Especially if I told her I had been watching her every day. I'd hate that — that's creepy! So, what would I say to her? That I liked her? How would I know that? I'm sure that's what she would ask.

Forget it. I won't write her at all.

I looked around the room. How long have I been here now? I thought. Nearly nine months.

The room was in disarray. The schoolbooks left untouched from Mrs. Williams' last visit. The mug of Ovaltine also left untouched, and cold from last night.

"Why study?" I groaned.

I peeked again. The boy was gone.

It bothered me all that day. I wondered who he was, what he was doing there, why he waved. After a while, I didn't think of it anymore. I turned on the radio. A perfect connection. A game in Detroit. Reno not in the lineup. They didn't say why. The Tigers went down to defeat. Lost it in the eighth inning. Jim Bunning had pitched a near perfect game. Where was Reno? Why didn't they play him? The team's top hitter. The one who was going to unseat the American League's top slugger. The legendary Ted Williams. Why didn't they play him? Maybe they would've won.

That night I decided to write to Ted Williams.

Dear Mr. Williams

I see the other day you threw a bat at the dugout. You were mad that you haven't been hitting so well. You have always been on the top, and you're getting older maybe, and maybe you're not as sharp. I don't mean to criticize you — it's just that you should relax a little. Like my friend Reno Bertoia of the Tigers. He must make you mad because he's so relaxed. Just goes up to bat and takes a swing at the best pitch, and it goes where it should. Base hit every time. Well, maybe not every time, but almost. He's relaxed, maybe like you used to be. But don't be mad at Reno. He's just doing what you have done all your life.

Reno

That next night, lying in the darkness, I knew the Tigers weren't playing, but I thought I might catch some other game. That's when I heard this voice. Rising and falling. A full, melodious voice. I heard the words "We have lost God. We have lost our anchorage, our moorings, our moral direction, our spiritual sensibilities …Give yourself to Christ. Come forward now. And as you come, many of you are not quite sure what is happening to you. It is a new birth. It is something God does for you supernaturally."

The voice was golden. I was spellbound.

Again the voice, "We need a spiritual revolution in America, and the place where it could begin is here in New York."

It was Billy Graham. At Madison Square Gardens.

"A sinful nation! A people laden with iniquity!" he roared.

That voice booming out over my plastic radio. Nothing like I'd ever heard. I was enraptured. I had never heard anyone so swaying in his words, so vigorous, so focused. I felt he was there in the room with me. Right there. I felt I could reach out and touch that voice — it was so real.

Maybe he could cure me. Maybe I could play hockey again.

CHAPTER TEN

IT WASN'T LONG IN coming. A letter from Boston's Fenway Park. My letter back.

"What's this?" I said to myself. "They sent my letter back to me with a photograph."

There was a picture of Ted Williams driving a homerun over the Green Monster. A massive homerun. His autograph: *"You doubt me? Just watch!"* Signed *"Ted Williams."*

I unfolded my letter. Scrawled across it in red ink was this message: *"Just wait!"* Signed *"Ted."*

My 12-year-old heart was pounding. It was as if the two of us were in the dugout and we had this conversation. My face was hot. I could feel the beads of sweat on my forehead.

It was the first and only response — real response — that I had had to my letters. Ted Williams had spoken to me! He had put out the challenge. I still thought he was washed up, that he wouldn't make it this year, that his average would continue to spiral downwards.

"I know you'll do it, Reno! I know it!" I whispered to myself in the silence of that attic room.

I sat for a long time, staring at the letter and the photograph of Williams. Admired that long stride into the pitch, how the ball must've risen like a missile to sail over the Green Monster. He was proving a point. Reno was no homerun hitter. He might end the year with a half dozen, but that wasn't his strength. His was getting the ball into play, pushing it into the open spaces, the gaps. He had good legs. A great glove. But Williams was legendary. The perfect hitter. His eyes bore down on each pitch. He could see the stitching. He could see the spin on the ball. He could predict whether the ball would slide or dip. At least that's what everyone thought.

But I still believed it was Reno's turn.

It was late afternoon. I sat by the window again. Could see the kids heading home after school. Thought I might catch Patricia. She must've stayed late. Then I saw him. That boy. A tall blonde kid who was across the street the other day. He was walking with others — boys whose names I had figured out from my dad's list. Suddenly, he wheeled around, but only for a second, and he seemed to be looking my way. Then turned back to his friends, and continued up the street till the gang reached the Shell Station. The boy finally separated from them, and headed down Hiram Street. He turned once again. He was by himself. Maybe I was imagining it, but he may have looked back at the windows, and me. Maybe he half waved. I wasn't certain.

Who was he? What did he want with me?

I don't even know his name.

That afternoon, I tacked up the photograph of Ted Williams. I had to move some of the pictures around. He went to the bottom of the list, though I must admit, I favoured him over Howe and Perry Como. I also tacked up my letter from him, just to one side of the pictures.

Now I had a rock 'n roller, a crooner, a jazz musician, a legendary ballplayer, the greatest goal scorer of all time, a newspaper photo of Reno, and that fellow from Detroit who they called Mr. Elbows, or the one who sold his soul to the devil.

What next?

I fell asleep and dreamed I had been to Madison Square Gardens. That I had been sitting there all alone when Billy Graham sat down beside me.

"Can I do anything for you?"

"Sure," I replied.

"Tell me."

"I want to play hockey. I want to be the best hockey player ever, and to play with the Rocket."

"Can't do that."

"Why not?"

"Because you have polio."

I woke up in a cold sweat, short of breath. My whole body was shaking. My legs ached. My head throbbed. The dream was so real. I expected when I opened my eyes, he'd be sitting on the bed beside me. On the night table beside my bed was a plate of sliced apples, now yellowed, and a glass of milk, now warm. My mom must've been up here a while ago, but I was asleep. There was a note from her: *Be back for supper! Had to run down to Orillia to pick up some things … Love, Mom.*

Alone again.

Dear Patricia

I see you every day. You seem very bright, very smart. I wish I could get to know you. Maybe when I am better, we can meet and talk. Every day you pass by my house, and if you were to look up, you'd see me in the window. I would really love to be out walking with you and everyone else. I have polio, but it isn't so bad. My legs hurt, but not every day. And the doctors say I will be in school come September.

Reno

I agonized over what I was now going to do with this letter. Send it like a paper airplane as she sails past the house?

"That's dumb!" I thought.

Instead, I pinned it up next to the picture gallery above my desk.

Chapter 11

The old monsignor was by again. He had dug out a clipping for me of Reno. His first at bat in 1953. The pitcher that day was the legendary Satchel Paige. Three swings. Three strikes. Out.

In the second inning, Bertoia went to make a play at second, but the runner spiked him flying into the bag. He got the out, but he was out of the game himself. His leg suffering a deep gash.

Not a good day.

I felt badly for Reno.

"Don't worry — he was just a kid himself. Barely 18. He survived. Look how well he's doin' now!" said the monsignor.

"Yeah, he's great, isn't he? Better than Williams."

"Well, he's chasin' him."

The monsignor stood at the top of the staircase. He studied the room. Didn't say anything for a moment or two. He seemed anxious. Then nodded, as if he suddenly understood what he had been wrestling over.

"You gotta pretty good setup here!" the monsignor remarked finally.

"Why haven't you sent that letter to Patricia?" he remarked after noticing it pinned to the wall.

"Oh, I don't know — she's, you know, I don't know, I guess I don't know her address."

"Well, see to it!"

I was surprised by the old priest's reaction. I figured he might discourage me. Usually that's the case, isn't it? Maybe he felt sorry for me. Who knows? I wished Patricia knew how I felt.

Still no word from Reno. I wondered why he didn't write back. After all, we had the same name. Besides that, Williams, far more famous than Reno, wrote to me. So why not Reno? I might change my name back. Be Henry again. Why was I fooling myself? I wasn't Reno. Everybody called me Hank. Mom and Dad did. Only the monsignor and Mrs. Williams called me Reno. And I hated her. I didn't care what she called me. I hated her.

She hadn't come that week. She was away, but the next week I will have to see her every day to make up for it. I dreaded the moment!

That day, no mail.

I was so discouraged, I didn't bother to tune into the ballgame. I didn't care any more. I had put so much energy into writing Reno, and he never once replied.

That night I didn't want to eat. I thought I should start reading more. I had snagged a few books from the ones my dad brought home in a cardboard box last week. Someone handed him the collected works of Mark Twain. Twenty four volumes.

My dad sat on the bed beside me last week and we talked about how I should be reading more books, not just newspapers. I told him I had read the Classics Comics version of Huckleberry Finn.

"That's great, but the book itself, Hank, is fantastic. I read it as a kid. You *must* read it!"

So I started the novel. Mostly because now I was sick of baseball. Sick of Reno Bertoia, too. *Why didn't he write?*

Mark Twain's Huckleberry Finn was nothing like I had seen in the comic books. I wished I could write like him. I fell asleep that night with the book on my chest. The glass of Ovaltine left untouched. Why did my mom keep bringing that to me?. Why? I didn't drink it? It was always there in the morning when I woke.

The next day I was resolved to write at least one more letter to Reno.

At first, I wasn't *really* looking for a photograph to put up on my wall — though that would have been nice — but now, I wanted one.

I sat in the window on my stool surveying the town. There was Paul, the cabbie. And Lillian. Meeting again like that. I looked the other way, into Mr. Bowman's yard. He was opening up the shop. There behind him was Mrs. Bowman. She was arguing with him. Her arms slicing the air. Gesticulating. He was shaking his head. I couldn't hear what they were saying. He finally turned to her, put the index finger of his right hand on her lips, as if to silence her, but she shoved it away. He opened the door to his workshop, stepped inside. Mrs. Bowman followed, but he gently pushed her back through the door, shaking his head, like she was crazy. He then slammed the door. I saw him bolt it. She banged on the glass. He walked off inside the shop. Disappeared from my sight. I studied Mrs. Bowman — her arms folded across her chest, fuming, her head turning to look back at the shop for a second before she marched back to the house. What was going on?

Later I saw the monsignor making his way downtown. In a hurry. Stopping first at the post office. Then wending his way to the Patterson Hotel. He paused there. He kept eyeing the street, then gestured with arms wide open, a little surprised. A woman with a tiny red hat approached. I couldn't see who she was. She sauntered right past him. I saw the monsignor look up and down the street. He straightened up, unfolded the newspaper he had been carrying, as if he needed to check something. By this time, the woman had disappeared into the hotel. The monsignor did one more check of the street, then stepped inside to follow her. What was going on?

Lillian in a tight skirt was on the main street again. Flirting with the road crew fixing the curbs. Idling about. Blowing a kiss to one of the fellows, and giggling. She finally sauntered off, offering one last glance. What was going on?

I heard the mailman drop something through the slot in the door downstairs. Mom was out again, Dad at the plant. This was happening more and more. Leaving me by myself. I must be getting better.

It took me a bit of trouble getting down the stairs that morning. My legs had hurt all night. I finally settled on the floor of the foyer. Bills, bank statements, a letter from the school and an envelope with no return address on it. But addressed to me.

This time, I didn't bother with the butter knife. I pealed away part of the flap, and ripped the rest open. My heart raced. Reno had finally written to me.

Instead a picture of Willie Shoemaker tumbled out of the envelope, along with a short note attached to by a paper clip.

Dear Reno

Thanks! Maybe next time I'll figure out what's what!

Willie

There was a snapshot of him on a horse. I'm not sure if it was the one from the Derby or not. Might've been.

It went alongside the others. Now I had a horse and a rider. I liked Willie. I liked that he made a mistake. I liked how things didn't turn out so good for him, at least not on that day of the week. He seemed okay with it. I liked that. Things don't always turn out the way you want them. So said Mom and Dad. They should know — they had me.

The polio kid with legs that didn't work right.

Maybe my luck was changing — famous people were writing to me.

Maybe not Reno, but others. It would happen. I was sure of it.

Chapter 12

I couldn't believe it. The newspaper had sat there for a whole day. I hadn't bothered to open it up. I had occupied every waking moment with Huckleberry Finn. Besides, I was tired of sports, and my newest hero was now Willie Shoemaker. I was probably his height. Maybe the polio would stunt my growth, and I'd wind up as a jockey. I liked him. I even told my mom that day I might change my name again. This time to "Willie." She scooped up the dishes in my room and marched down stairs without even answering. Just shook her head.

"I'm just kidding!" I shouted down to her.

"Okay, Hank!" she replied.

"My name's RENO!"

"Okay, Hank!"

I hated the name Reno now.

Until I opened up the newspaper to the sports section.

There it was — Reno had taken over the American League title. He was way ahead of Ted Williams. I was on my knees staring down at the newspaper spread out on the floor in the foyer. I couldn't believe it. Two hits in three times at bat in Boston.

Williams only managed one hit, but his average had been in steady decline. Detroit's hitting coach was ecstatic: "That boy just keeps chugging along like a train running out of Kansas! He's on first!"

By the end of that game, Reno was on top. Top of the American League in hitting. A .393 average.

I let out a whoop. That had my mother racing up the stairs from the basement. She shouted, "What's wrong? Did you fall? Are you all right?"

"Mom! Mom! Reno's top of the American League!"

"That's it?"

"Mom, do you know what that means? He's the best hitter in the American League. Better than Ted Williams. Better than anybody! I told Dad he'd do it! I told him!"

"Okay, okay, calm down! Do you want to call him? Do you want to call Dad on the phone — I'm sure he won't mind."

I did. We talked for fifteen minutes, or more. He told me I was right all along. Told me I must be intuitive. He said maybe this means Reno will stay on with the Tigers.

"What do you mean? Of course, he will! He's tops in the League. He's the next Ted Williams!"

"Oh, I don't know about that," my dad said, "Do you know what happened last year?"

I didn't.

"Last year, he started the year with a bang ... Maybe I'll write to the *Windsor Daily Star* and get Doug Vaughan — he's an old friend of mine — to get you the story he wrote from Opening Day at Briggs."

"What happened?"

"Well, as I say, Reno started off like a race horse out the gate. It wasn't the nicest day of the year. I recall — a blizzard! I couldn't understand how they could ever play in that weather, but they did."

"But what happened?"

"Well, I think he got a couple of hits, but he was great. Anyway, Hank, I have to go now, but I will send a Teletype to the Windsor plant, and get someone to ask Doug Vaughan to mail the story to you. He wrote it better than I could say it …"

I was disappointed. I wanted to know everything. Right now.

"Did he win the game for the Tigers?"

"Hank, I'm not sure — let's wait. I don't want to tell you something that isn't right."

"Okay," I said, feeling defeated.

My enthusiasm returned when I looked back at the newspaper. A tiny little story with the headline: *Reno Takes Over A. L. "Hit" Lead.*

I clipped the story, and pinned it up there with Willie Shoemaker's picture and the others. I moved Howe again. And Perry Como. I wanted the clipping next to the newspaper photo of Reno. He was my hero again. Willie was still pretty special, but Reno was the genuine article.

Yet part of me felt empty. Still no word from Reno.

I persisted.

Dear Reno

I know you are probably very busy, because it must be tough keeping your concentration, seeing as you are on top of the American League. Better than Williams. Better than anybody! I told you in other letters, I thought you would catch the old man! And you did! He's going to "eat your dust," as my dad said. You watch! You'll be there in September.

Reno, your greatest fan

It felt good writing to him again. I didn't expect anything back. That didn't depress me anymore.

I wondered again about Billy Graham. I decided to write him about my dream.

CHAPTER 13

DEAR MR. GRAHAM

I am a 12-year-old boy living up north in Canada. I heard you on the radio the other night. You have a beautiful voice, and you are a great speaker. I wished I could've been at Madison Square Gardens. I am not sure whether I would have given myself to Christ, or gone up there, like the others. Well, I couldn't, considering my state, or if I did, it would've taken me a long, long time. I have polio. I thought when I heard you, that maybe you could cure me.

The priest at the Martyr's Shrine said if I prayed the rosary every day, I might get better. I pray every night … Well, as long as I don't fall asleep, and more recently, I have been reading Huckleberry Finn and I fall to sleep with the book in my hands. But I do pray as often as I can.

I am writing to tell you about my dream. I dreamed you sat on the edge of my bed and asked what I wanted most. I told you I wanted to play hockey. You told me you couldn't help me because I have polio. What about a miracle? Have you ever performed a miracle? Could you make me better?

Reno

That night, my dad called up to me.

"Hank! Hank!"

I was getting ready to tune into another ballgame. I could hear him making his way up the stairs. He didn't come up there often. Mostly, he was at the plant, working late. He was still fighting the unions, and worried about the pending strike. And so he was at the office most days and nights, except for returning home for dinner.

"Hank," he said, "I have a surprise for you but I wonder if you are up to it!"

"What?" I said, perplexed.

"Tonight, I am going to take you somewhere ..."

"Another ride in your new car?" I said with a trace of sarcasm.

"Well," my dad hesitated, "Sort of, but that's not all — I thought we could go to the Palladium."

"The bowling alley?"

"Yes, it's a five-pin alley."

"But —"

My father cut me off. "Don't worry! I've rented it for us. For us alone. Except for the pin boys, but everybody's fine with it."

"Really, Dad, but I don't know how to bowl."

"Neither do I, but we can learn, and it'll be fun and it'll get you out of here!" he told me, as he surveyed the room. You spend too much time here!"

"But I like it here!" I whined.

"So, you don't want to bowl?"

"Oh no! I mean, yes I do. Absolutely!"

That night, we drove in his Studebaker. This time down the main drag, turned left at the clock tower of the old post office, and made our way down the hill to the bowling alley. The Palladium was just before you got to the tracks. On the west side.

"Just wait here a moment!" he told me. I stayed in the car. After a few moments, my father returned. He shoved his wallet into his back pocket, swung open the door, and helped me out.

"The way I figure is you can just hold the ball and throw it from a standing position — you don't have to use your feet or make that big stride down the alley. It'll work just as well. And I'll help you."

"Okay, sure! But I feel strong."

And I did. I hadn't played any sports for more than a year. I was determined to do well. I was also resolved that I wouldn't need any help. First, I wanted to watch my father to get the idea of the game itself. He scooped up a ball from the narrow rail. He then eyed the pins down at the end of that gleaming hardwood floor. Then with a quick stride, and long, long arms let the ball fly down the lane. A strike! First time! I cheered him. He slapped his hands together in triumph.

"Your turn! Beat that!"

I got to my feet, and it took me a minute or two to move to the long narrow rail. I scooped up one of those marble-patterned balls. I then bent down and swung it between my legs, three times, and let it fly. It took a bad bounce, but straightened up and careened down the alley.

"Strike! "I cheered. My arms raised in the air. I felt like dancing, and as I turned around to face my dad, I could see him cheering, but I lost my balance and toppled to the floor, my head hitting the hardwood. My father was at my side in seconds.

That's when I saw the boy again. He was gazing down at me.

"Ah . . .what , what are you doing here?" I stammered. My head throbbed.

"Are you all right?" he asked.

"Yeah, I am, but —"

"I'm a pin boy, and I was watching, and …"

"He's fine, I think," offered my dad. "Thanks for your concern."

"No problem," the boy replied. "My name's Billy. What's yours?"

"Hank!" my father said on my behalf just as I had opened my mouth to utter, "Reno!"

"Oh," Billy said, "Hank Reno!"

"No, just Reno!" I said, correcting my father and sending him a stern glance.

"Let me get some ice," my father said. "Will you be okay for a second?"

"Yes, of course," I said. And my father went to the manager to get a bag of ice for my head.

"Do you want to try again?" Billy asked.

"Sure!"

That night we played a few more rounds, but it tired me. My father agreed to call it quits. He was helping me out the door when Billy approached, offering his assistance.

"No, it's okay — I can do this!" I said proudly.

"Sure. When can I see you again?" he asked.

Both my father and I were surprised. I didn't know what to say. My father finally pointed out that I had polio, and that while most felt it was "catchy," it really wasn't, and besides, I was in its final stages.

My father turned to Billy and explained, "If you want to see Hank … er … Reno — Look! I call him Hank — you should probably ask your mom … How old are you anyway?"

"Fourteen."

"Well, ask your parents if it's okay, then you can come over. Do you know where we live?"

"He does, Dad! He knows."

"Fine then."

We drove back home. I had forgotten all about Reno. About the game tonight. It was probably nearly over by now. I really didn't care anyway. I savoured the name. Maybe a new friend. I lay in bed in the darkness, turning that name and over again in my brain.

Billy. Billy. Billy. Billy.

Chapter 14

I woke up the next morning, and Reno was still atop the American League. Day two. Still ahead of Williams.

I didn't even feel sore, after my fall, even though my head had a goose egg. And my parents had been up during the night to wake me a few times, fearing I might've suffered a mild concussion. I was fine.

I was eager to check out the box scores in the paper.

I saw the tiny box: *Leading Batsmen.* There it was. I had waited for this.

American League

	AB	R	H	Pct.
Bertoia, Detroit	88	11	33	.398
Fox, Chicago	89	18	34	.382
Power, Kansas City	64	10	24	.375
Williams, Boston	84	20	31	.369
Mantle, New York	77	18	28	.364

When I scanned the National League, Stan Musial of St. Louis was leading with Hank Aaron close behind. Musial was batting .375 with 39 hits and 14 runs swatted in.

Reno was king of the league! Too bad Detroit was in fifth place. Chicago was in first, the Yankees close behind, then Cleveland and Boston.

Day three: Reno still hot with the bat. Again against Boston. I listened to the game. Scratchy radio sounds dominating the play, broadcast from Boston. The signal not very strong, fading in and out.

It turned out to be a 2-1 decision for the Tigers. Right-hander reliever Jim Bunning was on the mound in the final innings. He fanned eight batters, including Williams three times. The Boston slugger marched back to the dugout, his bat held stiff in his hands like a club.

In the ninth, the "Splendid Splinter" as they called him sometimes, got some of the old luck back. The right fielder Al Kaline lost the ball in the sun, and it dropped in for a double. Williams was safe at third when the next batter popped up a sacrificed fly.

Jackie Jensen was up next, and slammed one down into the corner, scoring Williams. But Bunning got out the next two. Game over. When all was said and done, Reno had banged two singles in four trips. In the series in Boston, he had gone six-for-10.

I slept well.

When I woke, I was gazing across the room to my gallery of pictures. The faded Reno. The Rocket, and Gordie Howe, and Chuck Berry, Willie Shoemaker …

It was then I noticed the letter to Patricia was missing.

Chapter 15

I searched through my desk, all around on the floor. Maybe it had fallen there.

I had wanted to move it because Mrs. Williams was coming next week, and I'm sure she would have something to say about it. Correct the grammar. Or try to improve upon it — transform it into a letter with proper spacing and salutations.

But it was nowhere to be found.

I sat for a time at my desk, wondering if somehow I had put it away.

My mother ascended the stairs balancing my toast and bowl of hot oatmeal. I asked if she had seen the letter.

"Yes, I did. I read it!"

"You read it?"

"Yes, I did. I hope you don't mind."

"Well, where is it? I can't find it."

"Well, I have a little surprise for you — I mailed it."

"What!" I said alarmed. "You mailed it? When?"

"The other day."

My mind swirled in bewilderment. What had I said to her? Why had I kept the letter? Had I *really* meant for it to be posted?

"Mom!"

"What, Hank? Did I do something wrong? I thought you would be pleased. You didn't know where she lived, and so I found out from the post office. I took care of it — I thought it would be a pleasant surprise."

I said nothing. I brooded. My mind started re-writing the letter, or at least composing another to cancel out the first:

Dear Patricia:

I hope that whatever I said in that letter makes sense, and I hope you're not mad that I wrote it — whatever it was I wrote. Please forgive me. My mother mailed the letter. I didn't. Don't misunderstand me — I did want to write you. But I wanted to make it perfect. I also wanted to mail it at the appropriate moment.

I guess I just —

"Oh, my God! Mom, why did you do this?" I interrupted my thoughts.

Dear Patricia:

My mother's crazy! She took a letter I hadn't finished and sent it to you. You don't even know me!"

Again, my thoughts were broken by my unanticipated consternation over what my mom had done. I wrestled over the impending humiliation.

"Do you want me to go over there, to Patricia's parents, and explain?" my mom asked.

"Are you nuts?" I bellowed.

"Look, don't shout — I can fix this!" she assured me.

"Mom! No! No! No! Just stop!"

My mother gently put down the tray of oatmeal and toast and quietly and carefully descended the attic stairs as if some sudden and radical movement might blow up the entire house. Meanwhile, I slumped in the gloom of my misshapen room. Where was Patricia now? It was the weekend. I wouldn't see her today. Why was I so concerned? She didn't even know who I was. I had *never* even met her, yet there I was — running rewrites of these letters through my head: *Dear Patricia! ... Dear Patricia! ...Dear Patricia!*

I stared blankly out the window. Russ from the Shell station prudently placed a lit cigarette on the edge of the window sill before attending to a motorist who needed fuel. A big Buick at the pumps. Russ the whole time conversing with the man who I couldn't see. Actually, all that I could see was the man's arm resting on the window frame of the door.

It seemed ludicrous. Just Russ and this arm speaking.

Every now and again, the man's arm, or more specifically, his hand gestured to make a point. Russ never broke stride in this mundane palaver. He kept right on gabbing. Even when Lum Bailey crossed the road. The milk runs were done for the day. And Lum was gesturing to Russ who was now collecting some bills from the hand in the car.

Russ then wheeled around to greet Lum. They stood like that a moment. Lum was pointing in the direction of Bowman's house. I am certain they were speaking about the big blowout over there.

What happened over there anyway?

I moved my stool to get a better look at Bowman's shop. The "closed" sign was now in the window. Where did he go? Mrs. Bowman's car was gone. But Mrs. Williams' little Austin Healey was there. Parked just at the curb.

I looked back at Russ and Lum. Still jawing and shaking their heads.

The *Gazette* would provide some clues — you watch. Always did. Something like: *This past weekend, Mrs. Giles Bowman went to Orillia to visit her ailing mother. She will be there till the first week in June.*

Read between the lines.

I could see from my perch what really unfolded. I couldn't wait till next week when Mrs. Williams would return. I thought I might write her an anonymous letter, but it's likely she'd guess who it was.

But what would I say in such a letter? What business was this of mine anyway? I felt these were all my characters. Figures in a dollhouse. I could move them one by one into confrontations. Determine their future. Give them words, or lines to speak. Breathe gestures into their puny little bodies. Make them stand up, sit down, writhe on the ground, grovel. Make them dance and sing. Make them get down on their knees and thank their creator they are alive. Make them do things against their will. Make them live beyond their means.

I was their maker.

But what about Patricia? If I could've, I would have reached down and snatched up that letter from her delicate fingers. Or better still, tossed stardust in her eyes, and make her understand me, the feeble words employed to win her attention.

I simply wanted to be her friend.

I couldn't now. She probably had already read the letter. She probably had settled on the fact I was silly, pathetic and weak.

What was Mrs. Williams doing at Giles's house on a Saturday afternoon? His shop was closed. And Julie Bowman was away. I would like to have reached in through the windows of that house and gently moved both of them, like chess pieces.

What would be my next move?

Patrica. Patrica. Patrica. Patricia. I'm sorry.

Chapter 16

The metal sound of the mailbox, and the soft thud of mail on the hardwood floor below.

I didn't move. I was worried sick over Patricia. What would she say? Or think?

My mother finally called to me. "There's a letter here for you! I'll bring it up." I lay in bed. I watched the sunlight play among the leaves of the chestnut tree. I had long ago given up on Reno ever writing. I no longer wanted to think about it.

"It's from Windsor," my mom said.

My heart leapt. Reno. Reno. Reno has finally written back. The return address on the envelope however was *The Windsor Daily Star.* Doug Vaughan had sent his column from last year. And a letter.

Dear Reno:

Your dad asked me to send along a column I did from last year's Opening Day. I guess you're taken with this ballplayer from Windsor. Reno. He's good! Maybe underestimated in the league, but he's got all the tools. I'll be keeping an eye on him. Especially now that he's fired us all up here! I hope he can sustain this.

Doug Vaughan

In the April 16, 1956 column Vaughan had written how Bertoia's "sparkling all-around performance was enough to make you thumb your nose at the snow flakes and forget the cold ..."

I went on to read about how on that day the kid from Windsor was up early at 7, how he made his way down to the ballpark, saw the snow clinging to the velvety green grass, and prayed that he'd do well.

In that first inning, he breathed his warm breath on to his cold hands just before he went up to bat. On that first pitch, Reno rapped the ball into left field for a single. Opening day. He was on first. A rookie fielder.

Later in the ninth, he was back at the plate. The lead-off hitter. Took a fast ball and dispatched it like a missile that wound up crashing against the 400-foot marker.

"There I was," Reno was quoted as saying, "There I was on base but no one could get me home."

In the field that day, Reno was a master. In the 6th inning, with two out and two on bases, he went to his left and made an impossible out on a hard hit by Harry "Suitcase" Simpson.

I read Vaughan's story over and over again. Imagined Opening Day. Pictured Reno sliding effortlessly along the baseline to snag that impossible ball.

Still no word.

Late afternoon when I heard the doorbell.

"Odd — who's that?" I thought. And slowly made my way down the attic stairs. Called out, "Just a minute!" Again my mom was gone. Again, I was alone.

Billy was at the door. I could see his shape through the door's curtains.

"Billy!" I said as I opened the door.

"Feeling okay?" he asked.

"Sure — no problem."

"Can you come out?" he inquired.

"Sorry — I can't be in the sun for long."

"Then could I come in?"

"Sure, if … if you like. Yeah, c'mon in." I said nervously, and opened the door wide to let him by. It seemed odd to have him in the house, since I had never had anyone my age in the house. No friends at all. My mother was surprised, too, when she finally came home. That afternoon Billy had taught me how to play cards. Go Fish. Crazy Eights. Hearts. Old Maid. My mom made us sandwiches, and a pitcher of orange freshie. She sat close by in the other room, a tea cup on her lap. Read the paper. She looked happy. Relieved maybe.

Things were getting better. My luck was running good.

I sat at the kitchen table. Forgot the aches in my legs. Forgot the town, the attic perch, the goings-on, Reno, the batting title. Forgot it all. Nothing mattered more than this. This moment and these cards and Billy. He made me laugh. Made me concentrate on the cards. The Queen of Hearts. The Ace of Spades. I had never paid much attention to playing cards at all. Never interested me. There I was now, flicking these stiff brightly coloured cards onto the arborite table. My eyes sparkled with deliberation. My hands danced with these cards. I was *good.* Fast to pick it up. And my 14-year-old buddy was patient, anxious to please his new student.

We played till dusk. He telephoned his mother finally. Informed her that he was coming home.

That night I lay in bed. My mom rubbing my legs. I had learned so much, yet nothing about him. Who was this boy? Why did he like me?

CHAPTER 17

I FORGOT ABOUT Reno over the next couple of weeks. Mrs. Williams had not returned, as planned. I was ecstatic. I couldn't stand her. She had gone away with Giles Bowman to New Orleans, someone said. Or at least that's what I heard my father repeat to someone on the phone. He didn't care about being careful on the line — we were on a party line, like everyone in town. As my father said often: everyone was everyone's business. That's how stories spread.

That's also how I gleaned the town secrets. When my mom left me on my own, I'd pick up the phone ever so silently, and listen. If someone paused, and detected me on the line, and said, "Would you please hang up," I'd stand stone-still and I'd hold my breath until they resumed. Then I'd quietly put the receiver back on the hook.

Today's story in town was all Valerie Williams, my tutor, and Giles Bowman.

The lines were abuzz. Yet no one seemed to know what happened to Julie. Valerie's husband, George, however continued to work long hours. He ate his lunch alone and kept to himself. Or so said my dad to my mom one night at dinner.

Meanwhile, my parents searched for a new tutor. And my schoolbooks remained on the dresser in my room — unopened, ignored. Billy continued to stop by after school most days. We played cards. I helped him with a few school projects, pasting newspaper clippings into a scrapbook for class. I felt useful. I now had something to contribute. My mother was pleased. She plied us with oatmeal cookies from the oven. Large silver trays of them she'd put on the sideboard to cool. We'd peal them off hot, juggling them in our hands, and laughing. And she'd bark at us to wait till they cooled.

Those afternoons before school was out, and Billy would come over, I continued with my letter writing. James Dean and Sal Mineo and Paul Martin. It was Martin who wrote back right away. On official stationary from the House of Commons.

Dear Reno

It was so good to hear from you. A former Windsorite! And from my riding! I see, too, you have a big interest in one of our town's favourites — Reno Bertoia. I know him well. I also understand how serious this illness is of yours has made life uncomfortable for you all these months, but it sounds like you are improving every day. You will be happy to know, too, that we are making great strides in health care with the Liberal Government. This will benefit you and your family.

If there is anything I can do for you personally, please let me know. I am at your service.

Hon. Paul Martin

A photograph of him was included, signed: *To my good young friend, Reno, who has found his way north! And maybe will come back to his roots in the south! Paul Martin.*

Then the Sal Mineo fan club. I got a fat package from the organizers — a button, a 5 by 7 photograph and membership card.

I stared at Sal's picture for a long time. I started to believe I looked like him. I held the photograph up to the mirror on the closet door. Side by side with my face. Same eyebrows. Same eyes. I figured I could pass for him — I just needed to sculpt my hair down my forehead, and maybe get some curl. My hair was flat as a pancake, and too short. My father always cut my hair. Brush cut each time. I longed for a regular barber. To be like everybody else.

My gallery had grown: Maurice Richard, Gordie Howe, Louis Armstrong, Chuck Berry, Perry Como, Willie Shoemaker, Ted Williams, Paul Martin and Sal Mineo. I was now was a member of both the Chuck Berry Fan Club and Sal Mineo's. I pinned both membership cards to my wall.

What about the others?

That afternoon after class, Billy came by. My mother told him to run up to the attic where I was. I was embarrassed. He had never been up there. I had always come down. In those few weeks I had known him, we played mostly in the living room and kitchen. This — the attic room with the tiny windows — was my sovereignty, my place cut off from the world, I guess, and I am not sure why I didn't want Billy to see it.

There was Billy now. Hesitating at the top of the stairs, scrutinizing everything. It made me nervous. I noticed a small box in his hands. He finally turned to me: "What a great place!" Then leaned slightly out the window to look over the town.

"I can see all the way down to Miller's Garage one way, and practically to Willy's Park — actually I can see the trees popping up over the high school! Amazing!"

Now, I was feeling somewhat proud. As if I had engineered this. As if I had been the architect of this planned view of the town. I remained mute. Too apprehensive. Couldn't say anything.

"Hey, look what I brought for you!" Billy said as he strolled across the linoleum floor to my desk where I sat. He handed me the box, but didn't look at me. His attention was fixed on the gallery of photographs and clippings. "Ted Williams! He sent that to you?"

"Yes," I replied. "Yes."

"Incredible! All these people sent these pictures to you?"

"Yes."

I studied his face. A ruddy expression and luminous blue eyes. His blonde hair longish, and fanning down the back of his neck, almost lost in the flannelette shirt.

"This is amazing! The Rocket, Chuck Berry … Wow!"

I liked Billy, yet I knew nothing about him.

Finally I said, "Well … I wrote to all of them … I really … Well, I guess I just read about them in the papers and comic books and heard them on the radio, and thought, well, why not write to them …"

"You just sat down and wrote them letters?" Billy reacted incredulously. He said this without ever taking his eyes of the gallery. "You just wrote to them. What nerve!"

I felt nervous again. Felt I was being dissected.

"Do you think it was odd for me to do that?" I said timidly.

Now, I couldn't believe how vulnerable I had made myself by asking such a question. It just slipped out. So familiar and intimate with my emotions — the way I might be with my parents, or the priest or the doctor.

"No! No! I think it's great. I just thought … Well, you'd have to be awfully bold!" he kidded. "But I think it's great! Man! Look at all these stars! And you wrote to them!"

My wariness suddenly turned to pride.

Then I examined the gift box Billy had brought. It contained a balsa-wood model of a B-29. My heart sank. I knew I'd never be able to put this together. Then wondered if it was for me.

"For me?"

"Yeah, I thought it might help pass the time for you — I know the tutor is coming, and all."

"Well, thanks."

"Do you like model planes? I mean, putting them together?"

"Actually, I've never really tried doing this."

"I can help. We'll have to get some glue and set it up somewhere. Like maybe on your desk. Would you mind?"

"No, no, that would be fine."

Chapter 18

Over the next few days, Billy and I worked on the plane. Piecing it together. Then painting it from paint my mom bought at Vern's hobby store next to the A & P. I couldn't believe I had made this plane. I had never done anything like this before. It had always bored me, this kind of thing. Or maybe it was because I was so clumsy with my hands.

Billy was so conscientious and helpful and eager and enthused. And when he would leave, I would hold this B-29 between my thumb and index finger, pretending to fly it. I would zoom it over my desk as if the flat surface was a rice paddy in Korea, or an open field in Normandy during the Second World War. The plane would dip and dive and rise and fall again. I controlled its speed, its fuel supply, its movements. I charted its course, its targets. I was its pilot, its engineer, its commander. And as I drove it to extremes, I could see the eyes of the Rocket on the wall above, watching my every movement …

I hadn't looked at *The Toronto Star* for weeks.

My dad that night climbed the stairs to my room.

"You might want to look at this," he announced. "Reno's still in a battle with Williams."

I had forgotten all about him. My hero.

There he was. I couldn't believe it. His average had dropped dramatically. Now batting .360. Mantle above him. So was Power. Indeed, Reno had slipped to sixth place. Williams towered like the king of the hill. My heart sank. What happened? I had forgotten all about him. I had paid absolutely no attention to him. Hadn't even tuned into the games. Instead, I had been building this plane with Billy. I had been reading Mark Twain. I had also been writing more letters. They were going out now just about every day. But Reno, I had forgotten all about. I felt guilty.

"Reno, I'm sorry," I mouthed in the silence of my room. My father had gone back downstairs. He had been encouraging: "Well, he's still in the race."

"No, he's not, Dad! It's over!"

"Well, you're a great supporter!" he said sarcastically.

I sat there in the attic room. I had let Reno down. I had stopped praying for him. Up till then, Reno had always been in my nighttime prayers. All that changed with Billy's arrival. The card games, building the plane, doing the scrapbooks, watching television together … I had stopped praying.

That night I wrote another letter.

Dear Reno

It's been some time since I last wrote. I see Ted Williams has gone ahead in the race again. I still think you can do it! My dad tells me we should never give up on our heroes — and you're my hero! I'm not giving up on you! Never! Keep going with this. I am sure you can beat that old man!

Reno

That night I prayed God would help Reno Bertoia.

Dear God, Ted Williams has always been the best — it's someone else's turn, and why can't it be Reno Bertoia? He was an altar boy. He still goes to church. My dad told me that. So why not him? He's a good ballplayer. He can hit and catch and run. Please, God. Help him win the title!

Chapter 19

I heard the mail being shoved through the slot downstairs. Two floors down. Same time every morning. Thud! Four envelopes addressed to me. Bundled together with an elastic bind. More pictures. I scanned the return addresses. Nothing from Reno. And mumbled, "I guess not! I mean, I don't even pay much attention to him anymore — why would he write me?"

The first package was from Minneapolis. Billy Graham. Out tumbled a mess of pamphlets, and donation envelopes, and a glossy photograph of Billy Graham, the golden-haired prophet from the south. It was signed: *To Reno in Jesus Christ! — Billy Graham.*

I studied it for quite some time. I lay in bed that night, the cool breeze from the window washing over me. The memory of that voice. Its electricity coursing through my veins, its magic filling my limbs and my brain. I felt he had been praying for me. I felt he had touched my soul. I felt he knew about the terrible and painful nights that kept me awake, and kept my poor mom alert. I wanted a cure. I wanted to be normal. I wanted to race in the park at the end of the street. Why me? Why me? Where was my cure? Where was my answer?

Billy with the riveting eyes. The firm jaw. The golden hair. The golden voice.

Suddenly, staring at this image of him in the picture spooked me. Maybe, he *could* make this happen. The form letter said I was in his prayers, and he was sending help, and all I had to do was give myself over to Christ.

Maybe it was happening now.

"He sent me Billy!" I muttered. I sat on the floor of the foyer. "He sent me Billy!"

I couldn't believe it. Billy. My buddy. Blonde hair. Sparkling blue eyes. Squared off Dick Tracy jaw. He *looked* like him— like Billy Graham. This was my cure! It was true. Whenever I was with him, I forgot the pains in my legs. I felt normal. I felt ordinary. I felt like any other 12-year-old boy. Good strong legs. Strong arms and hands.

Normal!

Cured!

Yet I knew the polio was still there.

My mom had just come up from the basement where she had been doing the washing. I could hear the washer rumbling and shaking below.

"Hank, what's wrong?"

I must've looked misty-eyed. Stone-still on the floor. Listless. Transfixed.

"What's wrong?" she asked.

"Oh, nothing, mom!" I replied. "Nothing, really! I just thought — well, I just thought it was nice of Billy Graham to send me this!" I handed her the photograph of the southern crusading evangelist.

"That's so nice! You're getting quite a collection. I'm so proud of you!"

She didn't notice. She didn't recognize the similarities.

Billy *and* Billy.

She hadn't put two-and-two together. My soul mate. A doppelganger of the evangelist. His sign to me. The answer to my prayers. I had wanted a cure. This was it. A companion. A friend. Billy, *my Billy*, came out of nowhere. I had never seen him before. I still knew nothing about him. He rarely talked about his family. I didn't know whether he had brothers or sisters, or how long he had lived in this town. I knew nothing at all. It seemed whenever I'd ask something, he'd divert my attention. On purpose? I didn't know.

"Mom, do you know Billy?"

"You mean, Billy Graham?" she asked.

"No, I mean, Billy, my pal?"

"Well, of course — he's here every day practically. Eats all my cookies."

She laughed. She liked Billy.

"No, I mean, do you know anything about him, or his family?"

"No, honey. I never see his mom downtown. They're new, like us I guess. Why do you ask? Is there something wrong? You look worried."

"No, it's okay … I just thought, well, don't you think they look alike?"

"Who?"

"Billy and Billy Graham."

"Oh, I see what you mean … Well, they both have blonde hair... a firm jaw, not like our side of the family." She laughed.

"Maybe the eyes, mom?

"I guess so. I don't know. Maybe …"

"Well, I just thought …"

"Sure, maybe there's a likeness … Well, listen I got to get back downstairs. I can hear that monster rumbling down there. "The washing machine rumbled like a summer thunder storm. Or maybe the floors of the old Montreal

Forum when the Rocket skated out for the overtime period.

I sat there, poring over the picture. I couldn't believe it. I couldn't tell my mom what I thought. It alarmed me — this eerie semblance. I had to make a point of asking him more about his family. I had to get to know him better.

Yet I didn't — in a bizarre sort of way — I didn't want to upset this welcomed sorcery. Or whatever you might call it.

Chapter 20

I sat on my stool at the window, but this time, I perused my attic sanctuary. The pictures gleaming with the sunlight falling on them that morning. The gallery had evolved. Billy Graham was now side by side with Maurice Richard. I shuffled the pictures around. I liked Billy Graham. He had helped me. I knew that. In a curious way, he had helped. I couldn't tell anyone about this. Nobody would believe me. They'd think I was crazy. I certainly wasn't going to tell Billy about it. Billy, my pal, that is. But I might tell Billy Graham.

Dear Mr. Graham

I want to thank you for your letter, and the picture. I have that picture up on my wall. But I need to ask you if you really understood my request. I had told you about my polio, and how I wanted a cure. My polio is still with me, but I don't think of the pain all the time, and that's because I have a friend, my first, and only, friend in this town. He came here right after I wrote to you. And his name is Billy, too. As a matter of fact, he looks a lot like you, except he's 14, a little older than I am. But he looks so much like you, maybe the way you looked as a boy.

I know this sounds weird, but is that you? I mean is that your magic? Or is it God's magic? The funny thing is that ever since he came here, I haven't been praying — it's like I don't have to. I feel so happy. Is that wrong?

Reno

I sat on my stool. I was proud of my gallery.

The other day three other photographs arrived. I hadn't expected them, because it had been so long since I had written these individuals. Like Sugar Ray Robinson. No letter. Just a picture. Smaller than the others, with his name printed on the bottom. And signed: *"To Reno, sweet as sugar — Sugar Ray"*

There was also a picture from Jerry Lee Lewis. I loved the fast piano he played. I used to sit at my desk and pretend it was a piano, and I'd bounce around on my chair. Sometimes I'd try to stand but it was too wearing. But the tunes stuck in my head, and sometimes I couldn't sleep — they riled me. I could feel my feet dancing under the covers on my bed. I told him that in my letter, and he scribbled across the picture: *To Reno with the dancing feet among the bed bugs! Jerry Lee Lewis.*

The third picture was from Yul Brynner. A picture from *The King and I.* It was autographed. That was fine. I pinned it up anyway.

Late afternoon in the attic. Billy downstairs. Talking to my mom at the door. I could hear his shoes drop in the foyer. Then the sound of him padding up the stairs in his stocking feet.

"Hey Reno!"

"Yeah, Billy!"

He had some books under his arm. "Your mom asked if I would help you with your work … I know you don't want to do it, but I want to help."

I groaned. "Sure, I'd rather have your help than Mrs. Williams'."

The two of us sat together. It was like that every day for the next two weeks. Working side by side. He helped me with my Arithmetic, History and Geography and English. I knew I had to bone up on all this stuff, because of that letter from the school the other day. I hadn't read it, but my mom told me it was from the principal who was going to send over someone to test me. Otherwise, I'd have to repeat a grade. I didn't want that. Billy would be going into high school, and I would be going into Grade 8, if I passed.

"Do you think I have a chance?" I asked Billy.

"No problem — you're a smart one!"

"You think so?"

"Oh, yeah, you get things so quickly."

It was never like that with Mrs. Williams. I had always been defiant, rebellious. I loathed her. Maybe it was because she was so patronizing. Maybe it was because she treated me as if I wasn't so smart.

I had to find out about Billy. I could never get in a word edge-wise.

CHAPTER 21

I HEARD BILLY running up the stairs. "Did you hear about Reno?"

"No, what. What happened?"

"Hit one against the Yankees. A homer."

Why had I stopped listening to the games? Why had I stopped caring so much about Reno anymore? Was it because he never wrote? Was it because Billy had become my newest hero? I certainly wouldn't tell Billy, but I admired him. His easy-going attitude. His encouragement. He also never let me down.

I pored over *The Toronto Star* he brought up from the foyer. A small mention of Reno Bertoia, a reference to how he had briefly led the American League earlier in the season. He had now dropped to .295. Still not bad. On the other hand, Williams was still there, near the top, not king of the hill anymore.

"You seem disappointed," remarked Billy.

"Oh no, not really — it's just that I used to like him so much, and haven't paid any attention to him lately."

"Why's that?"

"Maybe all the studying — I have that test next week."

"The school test, right? Well, we'll have to bear down and get the work done, but I think you'll be fine, then there'll be more time for you to listen to the games."

We worked all afternoon. Billy was my teacher, mentor, examiner. He tested me. Corrected the tests, and handed them back, and tutored me some more. He had a gift, this friend of mine. He could transform the most complex things into the simplest terms. He opened up my confusion and gave it form. My mom was impressed. She couldn't believe a kid of 14 could accomplish this. Billy just shrugged. He said he used to help his youngest sister. And that was the first time he ever mentioned anyone in the family.

"You don't help her anymore?" I asked.

"No, not since she went to live with my father."

"Where's that? Your father doesn't live with you?"

"Oh, no, he left when I was six. I don't remember too much about it … I see him every once and awhile … And my sister lived with us till a year ago. I used to help her with her homework. My mom said I was so smart … I don't know about that — I guess things just come easily to me. I don't know why. I don't think I'm as smart as you though!"

I blushed. "When did you move here?"

"April."

"That's why I never saw you, I guess."

"Yeah, I used to see you up here in the window, and wondered why you didn't go to school. And so I thought, I'd like to meet you. I mean, I have other friends at school, and I still have that job on the weekends at the Palladium, but you, you, sort of … intrigued me."

"I did?"

"Yeah. Silly, eh?"

"No, I guess I must've seemed weird."

"Yup!"

We both laughed. This was the first time we had really talked. I felt like hugging him, but didn't. I felt so close.

Almost as if he were my brother. But I was an only child. My mother couldn't have children anymore, even though she had wanted more. I was it.

Now, there was Billy. My mentor. Best friend.

CHAPTER 22

MY DAD SAT AT the kitchen table that morning in June. Shaking his head.

"Can you believe that?" The paper folded out over the table. He poured some Carnation Milk into the dark black coffee. Stirred it up, clanging his spoon against the mug.

"This guy's going to be the next Prime Minister!" my dad continued.

"Yes, I saw that … I thought everyone was happy with what was going on," I interrupted.

"Well, I think we were," my dad said, "but this is such a surprise."

My father held up the newspaper. The headline read: *An Early Vote Expected.*

The news stories talked about the defeat of the St. Laurent Government by this buck-tooth prairie politician John G. Diefenbaker. He handed the Liberals an upset, electing 110 members. St. Laurent's following gave him 103.

"I wonder what's going to happen," my father mused.

"Is this guy any good?" I asked.

"Well, I guess we'll have to see."

I didn't say much more. My father was a Liberal, having always supported Paul Martin in Walkerville. I had heard Diefenbaker on the radio. He looked silly with the buck teeth, the wavy hair and jowls like an old St. Bernard dog. Still, I liked the way he spoke. Heard him on the radio one night. I had been twisting the dial, and heard these rousing words about Canada, and being strong, words about changing the way things were in the country. All politicians sounded like that, but this was different. He seemed to *mean* it. I wrote him at the time, and told him I'd love to see the prairies. Told him I'd seen the pictures, and couldn't believe the flatness, the horizon looming up like an apparition.

I didn't hear from him. That's probably because of the election. He actually had come to our town, too, but of course I couldn't get out to see him. My parents would never go. Dief spoke at the arena. I sat in my window that night and watched the cars pulling in for the rally. I heard the cheering. I saw the new Conservative leader stepping out of Roger Bell's big Buick. Bell was the big Conservative in town. He never ran for office, but did all the behind-the-scenes stuff there. Aiken was running in that election. I saw the man everyone called The Chief. He stepped out to a crowded front entrance of the arena. Waving. He had that goofy smile on his face. For a half a second, it looked like he turned in my direction to wave, but I knew it had to be to a gathering across the road.

That afternoon, the man, who wore a tweed suit, came from the school. "Henry?" he asked.

"Yes."

"Are you ready for this?"

"I think so."

"Do you feel up to it? I mean, with your health and all?"

"Oh yes."

The man then speedily set up at the kitchen table. He seemed attentive. He put me through a series of comprehensive exams, one by one. Tests in Arithmetic, History, English, Geography. One by one, working away with an HB pencil. True and false questions. Problem solvers. Maps to fill in. Sentences to correct.

I did it all.

The man cleared the table, stuffed the papers in a big briefcase, and bid my mom goodbye and thanked her for the cup of tea.

"You'll hear in a week or two. I think you son will do fine," he told my mom.

I was relieved it was over. I repaired to the attic. Fell asleep. And stayed asleep. Billy had come over to see how I had done, but went away when my mom told him I was lying down.

I woke in the middle of the night. The windows open. The moonlight telegraphing a pattern on the linoleum floor. I got up. Could hear someone next door. Giles Bowman had returned. Valerie Williams with him. Or at least, it looked like her. They were unpacking the car. I hated her all the more now that she had broken up that marriage. I hated anything like that. "How could she return here?" I mused to myself. "Doesn't she have any shame?"

I returned to bed. Lay there thinking about Billy and what happened in his family. Why did his father leave his mother? What would I do if Dad left Mom? How would I make out? They hardly fought at all. They might have tiny disagreements, but they never fight.

My mom always said it was because of reading Anne Landers. She said it was almost better than going to church: "She's so wise. She knows more than the priest. She's a married woman, and how would the priest know anything about this stuff? They've never been married. They don't know what it's like."

Was Mom right?

Chapter 23

The letter was waiting for me downstairs. My dad was holding it in his hands.

"Hank, what's this?"

"I don't know — is it for me?"

"It says the House of Commons, from the office of the Prime Minister. Did you write to Mr. Diefenbaker?"

He seemed embarrassed, a little distressed. He was afraid people in town might know his political affiliation. I wondered why that would upset him, but it did.

"It says the Prime Minister's office on it?" I asked rhetorically.

"Yes, Hank. Did you write to him?"

"Yes," I confessed sheepishly.

"Well ... That's okay, but you know how I feel about these things. Politics can be a funny thing. People judge you by such affiliations. I don't agree with it, but that's just the way things are. We have to be careful, what with my status in this town. I am the largest employer. You know that."

My father then handed me the envelope. I sat in the living room by myself.

Dear Reno

You write very well. You have a gift, and from the moment I read that letter, I could tell. I am sorry about the polio. But maybe some day you will stand on the prairies, like I do whenever I get home from Ottawa. I can stand there, and see the great sweep of the land, the wheat fields running high in the wind. I love it. And your letter makes me appreciate it all the more. I'd love to meet you if I ever get to your town. I was there during the election. I am sure there will be another, and when that happens, I may come back to your town. If I do, watch for me.

The Honourable John George Diefenbaker, Prime Minister of Canada

The letter surprised me. So did the photograph. And the inscription across the bottom: *To a caring young Canadian, Reno, with my best wishes for you and this country of ours — John G. Diefenbaker.*

I was also surprised by how quickly he had responded. Why me? Why did he write to me? He had so much to do in running this country. Why me?

I felt like taking down Perry Como's picture. I still didn't like him. I wanted to put John Diefenbaker's picture above everyone. I couldn't believe this — the Prime Minister of Canada writing to me.

My father came upstairs later. He smiled when he saw the picture. He wasn't angry now. He shook his head, and remarked, "He may be Prime Minister now, but not for long — the Liberals will kick his butt pretty soon."

"But Dad, he's such a good speaker."

"Oh, he's all of that. An old courtroom lawyer. He's good. But not good enough. Wait till Paul Martin takes over!"

"Do you think Paul Martin will be Prime Minister."

"Absolutely — it's his turn. You'll see!"

I stared at the gallery. Hockey players, baseball players, two politicians, singers, an evangelist, a boxer, a jockey, a movie star …

I mouthed a silent offering to them all.

I love some of you. I hate some of you. But you're all friends. You all had something to say.

That night, I went to bed early. Still light at nine o'clock. I could hear Russ at the garage. Rolling in the tires he had set up outside. Shutting down the pumps. Some nights I stayed up and saw the light on at the back of the shop. Many of the men from town would file into the garage. Dad told me they played cards in the back. And drank whiskey. The town was "dry" then, so they had to do it behind closed doors. My dad told me the police chief often joined the garage poker game. And the undertaker who used to joke with Russ because of his weight. He'd say, "Russ, I don't think I have a casket big enough for you. I'll have to bury you in your pickup!"

That night, I was happy.

Happy about the gallery, about my new best friend — my only friend.

CHAPTER 24

THE LETTER FROM the school.

My mother carried it into the kitchen. Set it down on the arborite table. Went to the stove, poured hot water into the teapot, let it steep for a bit. Then sat there daydreaming, gazing out the window to the backyard, to the first bloom of lilacs. I sat across from her, frustrated because she had not opened up the letter. I was worried.

"Mom, aren't you going to open it?"

"In due course, or maybe we should wait till your dad get home."

"No, mom! Now!"

Her fingers were red from washing clothes. She looked fatigued. She had me late in their marriage. She was now 43. She had been married to Dad for eight years before she thought about having children. She had had two miscarriages.

I watched her take a knife and with deliberate exactness open the envelope, slide this typewritten letter out, scan the correspondence, one eyebrow raised. She looked up, smiled: "Hank, you passed."

I was going into Grade 8.

There was another letter that day. One from Ingrid Bergman. In March, she won an Oscar for her role in *Anastasia*. Naturally, I never got to see the film, but I did see some photographs from it in the newspaper. She was so beautiful. I wrote to congratulate her, but long after she had won. The letter from her agent, or office, came swiftly. It was slightly bent from the mail handlers. I pinned it up with the others. The first woman in my gallery. It made me wonder why I had not included women in this gallery before. What about Audrey Hepburn? Or Rita Hayworth? Or Joan Blondell? Or Lucy Arnaz? My mom liked her. Loved her TV show.

I yearned for the movies, to sit in the Norwood with its art deco doors, the narrow aisles. I could almost taste the popcorn in the square red and white cardboard boxes.

Sometimes I'd stay up late at night, especially on Fridays and catch some of the old movies. I loved television. Never missed an episode of *The Honeymooners* with Jackie Gleason and Audrey Meadows. Or *The Millionaire*. I used to indulge myself in the fantasy of Mr. Tipton stopping by the house to give us a million dollars. And the *$64,000 Question*. I'd struggle trying to find the answers.

Yet in those spring months, I mostly listened to the radio. It was sad that *Truth or Consequences* went off the air in March, then *Counterspy* in May. But I had been caught up with the batting race. I had been caught up with the movie stars and the letters I dispatched all around the world. In those months leading up to the end of school, I had grown so much. I had sharpened my focus on what seemed important. Or at least on what I thought was important.

School was at an end now. Summer had arrived. I had stopped my window vigils. I had stopped listening to the radio. I had forgotten Reno. Had forgotten Patricia. Still couldn't figure out why she never wrote back. But I was glad she hadn't.

The end of school brought other good news. Doctor Black stopped by to give me a full examination. His nurse accompanied him, took some blood in tiny, narrow vials.

He advised my mom my legs were strong, and that I was making a full recovery.

Billy was over just about every day, but was now putting in more time as a pin boy. Said he could get me a job in the fall once I was back to normal.

I continued to send letters out. I continued to receive packages from movie stars, ballplayers, singers, comedians, politicians. I wrote to designers, asking them about dress shoes with pointed toes. I wrote to Elvis praising him for his sideburns, and he wrote back telling me to send a picture of myself once I was old enough to grow sideburns. I wrote to President Eisenhower asking for golf tips, to Nikita Khrushchev, Jack Kerouac, Vance Packard, and to the Boston Museum of Fine Arts about the Rembrandts they bought.

Letters were going out daily. The walls of my attic were now crowded with pictures and newspaper clippings. Billy helped me put them all up. He'd stand back in awe of what I had accomplished. Then started feeding me more names. I wrote to the Crest Toothpaste company, and got a picture of the freckled-faced girl with pigtails declaring, "Look, Mom — no cavities!" I wrote to Harry Belafonte, Maurice Chevalier, Joan Fontaine, Pat Boone, Phil Silvers, Dale Robertson, Floyd Patterson and Jack Paar.

Those were good months. I was on the mend. I was feeling good about myself. Billy stayed close. In fact, we stayed friends all our lives.

As for Patricia, she moved out of town in September. I never wrote her again.

That fall I went into Grade 8.

CHAPTER 25

THIRTY YEARS LATER.

A tall, lanky man sits in the examining room of the clinic at Met Hospital Cancer Centre. He's flipping through a *Sports Illustrated*, reading about Cecil Fielder, a homerun batter in Detroit. The nurse hands me his chart. I flip it open.

I see the name. *Reno Bertoia*. I smile. I'm standing outside the examining room. My nurse asks, "Is there something wrong?

"No, no, not at all," I say, and quietly open the door and step inside.

Reno Bertoia. Narrow face, long lean fingers.

The nurse has asked him to undress. He gets up, and is standing now in the corner of the room wearing only a hospital gown, tied up at the back. His black socks look absurd. He seems nervous. He is wearing glasses.

"Hello, Doc!"

"Hello, Mr. Bertoia! Please sit down a moment."

We sit and talk. He tells me about the problems he has been having. Bowel troubles. Blood in his stool. Pain. This has been going on for months now. His doctor has sent over the blood tests, and results of a colonoscopy and upper GI.

"I've got cancer. Colon cancer."

"Yes, I see that. Now, I want to do a quick exam, then we'll talk about treatment."

Over the next few minutes, that's exactly what I do. Then I ask him to dress, and meet me in my office at the end of the hall. It is there we talk at length. The treatment and its effects.

It's not pleasant. I'm to see him at the end of the week to start the treatments.

And when we're done talking, he strolls out of my office, then turns a moment to say he noticed this gallery of pictures on the walls — the movie stars, boxers, recording artists, the politicians, like Dief and Khrushchev, the hockey players, like Howe and Richard, and the ballplayers …

"Yes, quite collection!" I said lamely.

"Yeah, I'd say. I see there's Ted Williams up there!"

"That's right!"

"But how did you get these — and who's this fellow, Reno? Someone you know?"

I had changed my name back to Henry.

Before I could explain, he said, "Of course, I noticed the name, because as you know that's also my name … I don't know if you knew it, but I played ball with ... Ted Williams, or rather against him."

"With the Tigers, right?"

"And a few other teams. Got traded to the Senators and Kansas … but mostly with the Tigers."

"I guess I knew that …"

"You followed the game?"

"For a while I did."

The next day, I was sitting back in my office, a stack of files on my desk, and the nurse knocked quietly.

"I have something for you."

"What is it?"

"One of your patients dropped this off!"

I peered up over my glasses, and reached out my hand to take the brown envelope. I put it down for a second, shut the file I had been looking at, took my letter-opener and sliced open the flap.

As I slid a photograph from the envelope, I spotted the picture of this ballplayer. A young and healthy ballplayer. A kid really. Eyes bright and hopeful.

Reno Bertoia.

Signed:

To Reno from Reno

Reno Bertoia.